MARRIAGE MASQUERADE
Making a Family Series, Book Three

BARBARA MCMAHON

Chapter One

Gemma Green paused in the office doorway, holding a stack of files and letters. Her heart skipped a beat as she looked at her boss — Nikos Petropoulos.

She swallowed hard. He hadn't a clue she was watching him. As long as she was quiet, stood still, he wouldn't notice her. As usual, his concentration was fierce. He could tune out the rest of the world when he focused on one particular thing.

She loved looking at him. His dark hair was meticulously styled, but often became disheveled when he ran his fingers through it or came in from a windy day. At his dark straight brows, frowning now as he perused the spreadsheet. Over six feet tall, he stood a good seven inches above her own five-foot-six height. And every inch honed as if he worked out like a body builder instead of working in a high-rise office building in Manhattan.

The seconds ticked by as she studied him, memorizing every detail. How many times in the five years she'd worked for him had she done this? More than a thousand, she knew.

And in two weeks she'd be gone, she thought with a pang.

She nearly faltered for a moment. *It wasn't fair.*

Studying the spreadsheet before him, Nikos frowned as if he didn't like the totals. She wondered what he was reading— and didn't envy the writer. Nikos was ruthless in business. Which accounted for his meteoric rise in the company— through sheer ability, not nepotism.

During the afternoon, he'd discarded his suit jacket and loosened his tie. He rolled up his shirtsleeves, revealing his muscular tanned forearms. The snowy white shirt fit perfectly across broad shoulders before tapering to his waist. She couldn't see his eyes as he read, but their dark gaze never failed to cause a shiver down her spine.

He was a beautiful man, exotic and exciting in a way that had the office secretaries sighing whenever he walked by. But he was her boss, and Gemma always kept that thought firmly in mind.

Besides, since the fiasco with James, she'd sworn never to become involved with another man. Once trust had been shattered, it became impossible to rebuild. She no longer had confidence in her judgment, her perception of others. And it'd be a long time before she'd trust anyone again.

It was late. The rest of the staff had already left for the weekend. Gemma was ready to go as soon as she gave Nikos the folders. She allowed herself the indulgence of watching him for a little longer.

For a second, she wondered how he'd take her resignation.

He was a curious mixture of Western education and Mediterranean tradition, making it very hard to gauge his reactions. Their company operated more formally than many in the United States, the style set by their boss with his manner of treating everything rather distantly. Did he ever lighten up, she wondered suddenly.

She'd never know.

Dusk was falling, visible through the large windows at his back. The scattered lights from the windows of the other skyscrapers sparkled. She'd seen this expanse of Manhattan every day for almost five years. It felt familiar, like home.

She smiled wryly. Nikos would never approve of such blatant sentimentality. He was a tough, no-nonsense businessman first, last and always. As he expected his personal assistant to be.

And if she had emulated him, she would never have found herself in the fix she was in now. Too bad she'd learned that lesson so late.

"I have the analysis you requested, and I brought the McCaffrey file," Gemma said, putting an abrupt end to her musing. "Elise finished the dictation you gave her, and those letters are on top. If you sign them now, I'll post them on my way out."

Elise Templer had been Nikos' secretary since before Gemma started working for him as his personal assistant.

She placed the stack on his desk, relinquishing her own

letter of resignation reluctantly. She didn't know what he was going to say, and hoped she could hold on to her control until she was alone.

Resigning proved far more difficult than she'd expected.

He looked up and nodded, his dark eyes focused on her.

"You read my mind about McCaffrey. I found a discrepancy in the latest numbers Hank reported. I need to compare them with our earlier report in their folder."

She nodded with satisfaction. It had become almost a joke at first, when she'd started anticipating his needs. Over the past few years, however, they'd just accepted it as a part of their relationship. She knew the shipping business almost as well as he did, her ideas and thoughts usually paralleling his. And she always knew what information he needed almost before *he* knew.

"Does the merger still look promising?" she asked, perching gingerly on the edge of one of the visitor's chairs opposite Nikos.

She let none of her impatience or trepidation show. He'd get to her letter when he got to it.

Taking a deep breath, she held it a moment before letting it slowly out. It didn't calm her. So much for that theory.

Nikos tossed down his pen and leaned back in his chair.

"Yes. Though the rate of return may not occur as quickly as I initially thought."

He glanced at the stack, distracted.

Gemma swallowed and waited patiently. She wouldn't look at her watch again. Doing so wouldn't change the pace of time.

Nikos reached out and lifted the first of the letters, tilting it as he quickly read. When he finished, he scrawled his signature and tossed it aside, picking up the next. In only a couple of moments, he'd signed the lot.

He pushed the folders aside and spotted her letter. With a quick glance in her direction, he picked up the envelope and withdrew the single sheet.

Gemma studied him quietly as he read, vowing she wouldn't cry, even though she felt the threat of tears. It was her decision, the only one she felt she could make. But it hadn't come easily.

She owed Nikos a great deal. She'd learned so much from him. He'd talked her into taking night courses until she got her degree, made sure she understood all the regulations governing the shipping industry and freely shared his own thoughts about the business. He'd made her job interesting and exciting and rewarding.

She enjoyed working with him despite the long hours and the hectic pace he set. She'd miss being his personal assistant. Miss living in New York.

Too late now for regrets. Months too late.

"What the hell is this?"

He looked up right into her eyes, his own narrowed.

She cleared her throat. "My resignation."

He stared at her for a long moment with the full force of his dark eyes, then he slapped the paper down and rose. Gemma watched as he strode to the window and gazed out over the busy street below. Leaning one shoulder against the glass, he slipped his hands into the pockets of his trousers.

As the silence stretched out, Gemma's mind wandered. She studied him, taking in the tall, lean frame. Memorizing as much as she could. A London tailor made his clothes. The dark somber colors and continental style did nothing to distract from his innate masculinity, his dark good looks.

Should she say something? Try to explain?

That would be dumb. The entire reason for leaving was to avoid explanations and excuses she knew would result once people knew she was pregnant.

And deserted by the baby's father.

She couldn't endure the pity or the gossip. She had to leave, and soon. Because at four months pregnant, the extent of her folly was about to be known.

Gemma knew Nikos would demand some kind of explanation. She shifted in her seat to gather up the signed letters, quickly folding them and inserting in the accompanying envelopes. Elise had made copies earlier. These were ready to be posted. She'd drop them in the mail room before she left.

Glancing at her watch, she saw it was after seven. Still,

someone was on duty in the mail room until eight. The letters would go out late, but at least they'd go out today.

"Is there anything else you need?" she asked, longing to escape.

Wishing she was already home. Wishing even more that she hadn't been put in this position at all. She didn't want to leave, yet felt she had no alternative.

"You could start by explaining that letter."

"I'm leaving New York," she said to his back.

"Going where?"

"I thought California."

It was as far from New York as she could go.

He turned at that and stared at her in surprise.

"Why? Joining some man?"

Heat stole into her cheeks and Gemma looked away.

"No. There is no man."

Not now. And in reality, never. She'd been such a fool.

"Then why? I know your parents are dead. You have no other relatives, right? What is the allure of California?"

Startled, Gemma looked up. Nikos' dark brows were straight as he frowned. He was angry. She recognized that instantly. She could practically feel waves of energy emanating from him—which was totally unlike the normally cool, controlled man she'd worked with for so long. Businesslike and contained, that was Nikos Petropoulos.

She'd always admired that. And had done her best to be

the same way. To be the perfect personal assistant.

Did she owe him a full explanation? She hated to see the disappointment in his eyes. He didn't suffer fools gladly, and what she'd done was beyond foolish. Of course, he didn't have a very high opinion of women to begin with, thanks to his wife. Ex-wife, she corrected herself.

So her own circumstances would only confirm that opinion.

When she'd started working for him, Nikos had been married to a renowned British super model. But that union hadn't lasted long. Katrina had been beautiful, elegant and sophisticated, but also greedy, conniving and unfaithful.

He'd divorced her three years ago.

Since then, he'd played the field, never drawing close to any woman. And sometimes his remarks the day after a particularly trying date demonstrated to her he didn't think highly of her gender.

"Is it something wrong with your work here?" he asked.

She shook her head.

"I think it's time for a change. I need to leave New York."

Rubbing her palms nervously against her long black skirt, she tried to remain calm.

"Leave New York? Why? Is it too expensive? Do you need more money?"

Gemma flashed him an indignant look.

"No, and if money were the issue, I'd list all I've done

during the past year and let the record speak for itself."

He stifled a smile at her flare of temper.

"It was unusual for you to advocate for yourself before. You know your work is excellent. You miss nothing, Gemma."

Warmth spread through her. She smiled in genuine pleasure and wry amusement. He could have volunteered that information earlier. But it probably had never crossed his mind to do so.

He glanced at the letter again, a thoughtful expression on his face.

"I need to get this resolved," he said slowly. "Your timing couldn't be worse."

"There is nothing to resolve. I'm formally giving notice. I'll leave in two weeks."

"Do you have another job?"

"Not yet. I need to move and get settled first."

He crossed to the desk and leaned against it, looking down at her.

"Tell me what's going on, Gemma. You're moving across the country with no job, no family, nobody waiting. What's the deal? You owe me an explanation, don't you think?"

Did she owe any man anything?

Twisting her fingers, she looked at them, wondering what to do. She just wanted everything to go back the way it had been, but that would never happen. Everything was changing, out of control. She wondered if she could cope.

"I'm pregnant," she blurted out.

Silence.

She ventured a glance to find his dark gaze steady on her.

"And the father doesn't live here in New York?"

"Oh, yes, he does," she said bitterly.

"Then why are you leaving?"

"Because he wants nothing to do with his child."

She raised her chin, drawing her pride around her like a cloak.

"I don't want people to know how dumb I've been. I thought if I moved away, I could pretend to be a widow or something. No one would know my baby doesn't have a father willing to acknowledge it."

"Good grief. Isn't that drastic? Moving away from your friends, your job? You wouldn't have any kind of support network."

"I can manage. I've saved some money, and I know I can get another job."

"Single women have babies all the time. You don't need to move clear across the country," he snapped.

"Maybe single women have babies, but it's tacky to be an unwed mother in my hometown. Small towns in Ohio frown on that kind of thing. And I didn't realize how much of those values stuck. I've lived here for years, but still feel...I don't know, embarrassed, I guess, is the least of it. And a certain amount of shame. I'd hate for my baby to know his daddy didn't want him. Or her."

"So you plan to keep the baby?"

Gemma nodded.

It was odd. With all the anger she felt toward James, she thought that some of it would have transferred to the baby, that she might even come to resent the child. But she already loved this infant growing beneath her heart.

Gemma had no family. Once her baby was born, it would be the two of them against the world. The thought of that precious new life was the only bright spot in her day. Despite the complications of an unexpected pregnancy brought, she was looking forward to holding her baby.

"Who's the father?"

"Just a guy."

"I don't buy that, Gemma. You aren't the type for casual sex. Who is he? That James you've been quietly dating for a year?"

She shrugged, a bit annoyed by the inquisition. Then nodded.

"I thought he was wonderful. Bright, funny, charming. I really enjoyed being with him. I thought I loved him. He said he loved me. But I know better now. I'll never trust a man again."

Or her own judgment.

She had been confident in the feeling of being loved. How could she have been so wrong?

"He heard about the baby and left?" Nikos guessed shrewdly.

"Two months ago."

"Want me to track him down and make him marry you? Or at least provide child support?"

She widened her eyes. Nikos could do it if anyone could. Slowly she shook her head.

"No. In the first place, I wouldn't marry him now if he were the last man on earth. Not that I could. He's already married—has been for years. A minor little detail he conveniently forgot to mention to me. I was just on the side, so to speak."

Tears threatened as she remembered how ashamed she'd felt when James had told her the cold, hard facts. How ashamed and scared and furious.

"Gemma—"

She jumped up.

"Don't say anything, Nikos. I know I was an idiot. But you don't have to worry I'll repeat that dumb mistake. I have to do what's best for me and my baby, and staying here isn't an option. I've really enjoyed working with you."

Backing toward the door, she tried to keep a bright smile on her face, but from her trembling lips, she knew she was failing.

Nikos watched Gemma as she bid him goodnight. His gaze continued to follow her as she entered the outer office.

Her thick chestnut hair caught back in a long ponytail at the base of her neck was tidy, even after a full day at work.

She always appeared immaculate. Slender, perhaps too slender, she dressed conservatively. Mostly in black and silver, he noticed.

Today, her black skirt swayed seductively against her long legs as she walked away. It hit her mid calf, a soft feminine garment. She had fastened her silvery blouse to within two buttons of the neck, but it displayed the generous curves that enhanced her femininity. The gold necklace that nestled against her throat warmed the honey tones of her skin. Beautiful, confident, poised—he admired all those features in his personal assistant.

Almost as much as he admired her business acumen.

She didn't look pregnant. How far along was she?

Surprised at the turn of events, he shook his head. Timing was everything—and he'd just received a second major blow.

Never in all the years she'd worked for him had Gemma been anything but totally professional. He'd taken her for granted, he realized. She'd been the perfect personal assistant. He couldn't even remember their first few months together, but he knew they must have been awkward. There had been so much for her to learn. But she'd caught on faster than anyone he'd ever worked with.

Gemma had quickly become invaluable to him. Since talking with the legal department, he'd wondered if Gemma could prove equally valuable to the company—managing it in his absence?

He frowned, not even wanting to imagine giving into the inevitable. He had time, a week at least.

Frustrated with the turn of events, he moved back to his desk. He came from a family with strong loyalty, unbreakable family ties. How could a man betray his wife by having an affair? And especially betray someone like Gemma? His own family was large, but close. He'd do anything for them. They had only to ask.

Nikos often felt Gemma would do the same for him, which was rare in employees these days. Was her loyalty to the company or to him alone? Could he keep her on board? If his own situation didn't improve, this would be the worst time for her to leave.

Her resignation was not an option. He had to convince her to stay. To hell with what people thought. She was a colleague, a close confidante, as well as an employee. Her departure would end that.

Nikos refused to even consider the idea.

He didn't need this added problem. The documents delivered earlier reclaimed his attention. His visa had expired. Someone on the legal staff had screwed up and not applied for the extension when it was time. Now he had to figure out how to fight deportation.

He was in the midst of negotiations for new contracts

with the longshoreman's union. Had just completed the buyout of a small domestic shipping line. Merging that into the parent company would also take time and his skills. He couldn't afford to be gone for a week, much less the months it might take for him to return to Greece and wait for a new visa to be processed.

He wasn't giving up. It'd take thought and an innovative strategy to address the problem. The problem was time was running out.

Hearing a noise in the outer office, Nikos looked up.

Gemma.

Blast it. He was slow today.

Why hadn't he thought of her immediately? He quickly crossed to the door.

Gemma had gathered her purse and the tote that held her dress shoes. She'd already changed into low walking shoes for her trip home.

"Did you need something?" she asked.

"Come back in for a moment, Gemma. I may have an answer to our problems—yours and mine."

He waited until she'd placed her things on her desk and walked toward him before continuing.

"Yesterday, the US Immigration Department served me notice. My visa expired some time ago, and Phil Mannering in legal failed to ensure its renewal. I'm being deported back to Greece."

Gemma appeared stunned.

"Can they do that? You run this place. Can't you get an extension or something?"

"Apparently, your federal law is such that citizens in my country need to be living there when applying for a new visa. Since the old one expired, I am required to apply for a new one. Had the current visa been extended before it expired, I wouldn't be in this fix."

"How long does that take to renew?" she asked.

"I can't renew it at this stage. I need to apply for a new one. And that will take at least several weeks. Maybe longer. I don't know where the United States stands with quotas from Greece. I've had that visa for so long I don't even remember all I had to go through to get it initially. And who knows how much more red tape there is now in that massive bureaucracy?"

"Can't Allessandros help? Doesn't he have some pull in Washington?"

Nikos' cousin, Allessandros Petropoulos, visited the United States for several months every year. His wife was originally from Washington, D.C., and now his family split their time between their two homes.

"I called him as soon as I found out. He's looking into it. But unless something comes up quickly, it'll be too late. I'm scheduled to depart next Friday."

Gemma leaned against the doorjamb and stared at him,

her mind whirling as she wrestled with the problem. At the moment, the challenge reminded her of countless other times when they had discussed impossible situations. This was serious.

"I don't know what to say. I know nothing about immigration laws and procedures."

"I believe I've come up with the perfect solution," he said easily.

Nikos looked just like he did when making a huge coup in business—arrogantly confident, supremely assured, and a bit like the cat who swallowed the canary.

"Marry me," Nikos said.

"What?"

The room seemed to whirl around, then dimmed. For a moment, Gemma thought she might faint. Only the pull of Nikos' dark eyes held her, anchored her.

Was she hallucinating? Had he just asked her to *marry* him?

He stood close enough she could see the depth in his eyes, notice the fine lines that radiated from the corners.

"At least consider it before raising objections," he said. "I haven't worked out all the details—we can do that together. But I believe this will work. You wouldn't be an unmarried mother and I'd make sure you didn't go through this pregnancy alone. You'd be my wife until I get permanent residency. Longer if it works out. We can each provide the other something we need."

She shook her head, unable to tear her gaze from his. Her heart pounded, and she tried to think. But her emotions threatened to overwhelm her. Nikos wanted to *marry* her? As in kisses and living together and—

"It's the perfect answer," Nikos said. "You wouldn't have to quit your job. You can continue to work as long as you feel like it."

"And after? When the baby is born and you have your residency, then what?"

Amazed that her voice sounded so normal, Gemma still leaned against the doorjamb.

"We'll see how things go. We can get a quiet divorce. I'll make sure you are adequately situated financially."

"I don't need your money," she said hotly.

Did he think he could buy a wife? That she was so desperate she'd consider such a move?

"Fine, then. I'll establish a small trust for the child."

"It won't work," she said.

The last thing she wanted to do was depend on a man for anything. Too much could go wrong with this idea. Just thinking about it had her heart racing, her knees wobbling. She couldn't possibly consider marrying Nikos.

She didn't possess the same level of sophistication as the women he usually dated. And before much longer, she'd be as big as a house. Was he seriously proposing that she become his wife to save him from deportation?

There must be fifty thousand women in New York City alone who would jump at the opportunity.

"Why me? Why marriage?"

"A marriage of convenience is not unheard of," he replied. "People marry for expediency all the time. It's not at all uncommon to find arranged marriages throughout Greece. Often the families of the couple arrange the alliance.

A marriage based on mutual respect and common interest will work, Gemma. On paper we'll be married, and in reality little will change. You'll continue to work as my personal assistant as long as you can. After the baby is born, we'll separate, sever the legal tie. But I'll keep your job for you."

"You can't marry merely because you don't have a current visa," she protested, dazed at the thought.

Though wary of his suggestion, the idea was growing stronger in appeal. She wouldn't be an unwed mother. Wouldn't have to worry about gossip and feeling shame and moving clear across the country when she really loved New York. She wouldn't have to leave Nikos or her job.

His features tightened slightly. He narrowed his eyes.

"I wish to remain in America. To leave for even a few months would be inconvenient. The idea has further appeal—I attend many functions during the year, and it's awkward to go alone all the time. And if I wish to reciprocate, I need a hostess. So you see, it'd benefit me in other areas to have a wife."

She stared at him. Realization gradually seeped in. Here was another man barreling through life at her expense, just as James had. Nikos wanted a marriage in name only, not because he cared for her, but for his convenience.

But what about *her* convenience?

He tilted his head, watching her.

"What's your answer?"

"I have a choice?" she asked.

She should stick with her original plan.

Only…the thought of relocating was overwhelming. It'd be far easier to stay where she was, have adequate help while she needed it, keep the job she loved.

"You may decline," Nikos said, his expression giving nothing away.

The coolness in his tone let her know he wouldn't be pleased if she refused.

Another thought flashed through her mind—if she didn't marry him, he'd likely turn to someone else. Which would leave Gemma no choice but to move.

Or you could stay.

Why not accept, she thought frantically. James had proved how fickle love could be. She didn't plan to fall in love again, ever. She'd make her career the most important thing in her life—after her baby.

Would marrying Nikos help in that regard? Probably. So why not a temporary marriage of convenience?

"What about my baby? Would you truly be willing to let people think it's yours? What about when we divorce?"

She surprised herself with how calm she sounded. Maybe he couldn't hear the pounding of her heart, the blood thundering through her veins, almost drowning out her own voice.

"The baby is yours. While we are married, I will let people think it's mine. When we separate, I'll provide for the child. I believe that's more than fair."

She nodded. He must really want to remain in the States to give so much to another man's child.

What was she thinking? They had nothing in common. He was a wealthy Greek shipping magnate. She was the daughter of a small-town banker. Was he crazy?

Or was she to even consider saying yes?

Just then, she felt a fluttering deep inside. The baby was moving again. She wasn't alone anymore. She had her child. And needed to do the best she could for that child.

"This arrangement will suit us both," he went on. "I think Americans have a peculiar romantic view of love and living happily ever after. Arranged marriages often prove extremely successful. I believe this choice is better than your plan. You're what—twenty-seven?"

"Twenty-eight."

Her birthday was three months ago, and he never acknowledged it, she thought wryly. Would anything change with a marriage license between them?

"Why uproot yourself on the chance of finding a good job on the West Coast when you have a good one here? Stay here where you can continue living the life you've made for yourself."

"Would I keep my job when we annul the marriage?"

"We work well together. I see no reason to change that."

He crossed to his desk and riffled through his appointment calendar.

"If I get Elise to reschedule some of next week's appointments, we'll have time to get married and notify Immigration before Friday. I'll have Mannering get to work on everything first thing on Monday." He looked up. "Does that suit you?"

"I'm not sure this is such a good idea."

There was no way she could marry Nikos Petropoulos. Why was she even discussing the matter?

His gaze caught hers, but he kept silent, as if the sheer force of his personality could convince her. The effect almost knocked what little sense Gemma possessed right out of her head. He looked incredibly assured, determined, sexy.

Sexy?

She *was* losing her mind. The last thing she wanted was involvement with another man. She'd learned that lesson well. This had to be a case of spiking hormones.

He studied her for another moment.

"At least I know up front you're not marrying me for my money or with some false declarations of my undying love. That will save a lot of heartbreak later."

"I never said I'd marry you at all," she protested.

How like the man to just declare what he wanted and assume she'd fall in with his plans. Swallowing hard, she tried to focus on the possibility. It proved impossible.

"So say it and end the suspense. I don't have a lot of time here, Gemma."

She swallowed again and opened her mouth. Then shut it. Sanity took over. She needed some time to consider his outrageous idea, no matter how short he was on the commodity.

"I need to think this through," she said.

Would he kiss her as her husband? Expect more from her than she could give? Or would it be a paper marriage only? Just an appeasement for the US Immigration Department?

And a way to save face for her?

That alone should have her leaping at the chance.

He nodded. "I can understand that. Until Monday, then."

Gemma hesitated, wishing he'd say something else, something that gave her a clue what would truly be their best course. But he seemed to have accepted her request and already turned his attention elsewhere as he picked up the spreadsheet in front of him and began to review the numbers.

Gemma left, still feeling dazed. She couldn't concentrate on anything except the echo of Nikos' words, *Marry me.*

Chapter Two

Gemma slept very little that night. She tossed and turned, tried to consider all the ramifications of marrying her boss compared to those of not marrying him. It was a futile endeavor. She couldn't keep a coherent thought straight for more than ten seconds. Her thoughts spun.

She had been determined to move for weeks, ever since she had finally admitted to herself that James would do nothing to help her. She'd started packing, had lined up a moving company, told her roommate she'd be gone by the end of the month.

Now she was supposed to consider an alternative.

She tried to envision life as the wife of Nikos Petropoulos, but simply couldn't. She didn't have the background or training to move in his exalted circles. Couldn't imagine living with him away from the office. Exchanging personal information.

Yet the thought was tantalizing. He'd fascinated her for years.

She wouldn't expect Nikos to take on the role of doting

father. But his willingness to let others believe the child was his touched her.

She wouldn't mind the rest—later. Divorced mothers were everywhere. When it came time, she could manage that. At least she thought she could.

And there was always California.

But was she being fair to Nikos? She'd reap far more from this temporary marriage than he would. He could put up with the inconvenience of waiting a few weeks while a new visa was being processed. Did he have to marry? Weren't there other better alternatives for him?

Finally, giving in to her restlessness, she rose and took a long shower. Dressed in faded jeans and a snug top, she brushed her hair until it shone, then pulled it back into her normally neat ponytail. Dressed for a day at home, she headed for the kitchen.

Though she longed for coffee, Gemma dutifully drank herbal tea instead. She could no longer consider only her own wants and needs. She had to ensure she properly took care of the baby. Preparing a couple of slices of toast, she loaded on the strawberry jam and sat down.

Drawing a pad from the counter, she sketched a chart and listed the pros and cons of Nikos' unexpected proposal.

But concentration continued to prove impossible. All she could think of was his dark gaze. The shimmering feeling of anticipation that seeped into her every cell when he turned those dark eyes on her.

She attempted to picture him sitting opposite her at the breakfast table.

Impossible.

She closed her eyes and tried to envision herself in the social whirl. He attended opening nights and special showings at the museum and art galleries. His cadre of friends included the heads of many major companies and some English aristocracy. What would she talk about to people like that? She was terrible at small talk. Business discussions, okay, or even girlish confidences she could handle—but nothing suitable for the circles Nikos moved in.

Shaking her head, she finished her meager breakfast and wandered into the living room. Her roommate was away this weekend. Susan was trying so hard to be supportive, but she really hadn't come up with a sound plan to convince Gemma to stay. What would she say to Nikos' bizarre proposal?

She'd still be moving from the apartment. Her heart skipped a beat when she wondered what his home looked like. Then a kaleidoscope of images flashed through her mind's eye, ending up with him drawing her into his arms and kissing her.

Oh my goodness, she thought, *what will I do if he kisses me?*

Which he probably would at the wedding ceremony, at least. Wasn't that part of the ritual?

Flushing, Gemma wondered why she fixated on a kiss.

There were a million other things to think about.

She checked the clock. It wasn't even eight. Pacing the small room, she tried to make sense of her tumbled thoughts. She couldn't. Maybe she'd go talk to the man. Get everything straight, understand exactly what their marriage would entail. Then maybe she could make the right decision.

That decided she wasted no time. If he wasn't at the office yet, she knew he'd be there before long. But when she signed in, she saw Nikos' name boldly written two lines above. He was already here.

Swallowing her trepidation, she turned to the elevators. Only on the ride up did she realize she was wearing jeans that had seen better days, scuffed running shoes, and a top that had been designed more for comfort than style.

"Just shows I'm not thinking straight," she murmured in the empty car.

When it opened on her floor, she hesitated. Maybe she should return home and think this through a bit more.

And change her clothes.

She ignored that thought, then stepped out and quickly made her way to her office. If she went home, she might lose her courage. Dropping her purse on her desk, she didn't pause but continued to Nikos' door. It stood ajar. No need to shut it for privacy when he was the only one here.

"Nikos?" she said.

He looked up, laid his pen down and let his gaze travel

from her face, slowly down her body and back up again. Gemma almost squirmed when he seemed to linger on her breasts and the snug fit of her top. She definitely should have changed.

"I didn't expect to see you today. Come in."

He rose politely.

For a moment Gemma hesitated. His proposal still echoed. For once she didn't see him as her boss—but as the man she might marry. He'd be her husband.

Stepping into his office, Gemma felt decidedly under dressed compared with his dark slacks and dress shirt. Granted, he didn't wear a tie, had his collar buttons undone, and rolled up his sleeves, but still, didn't the man ever relax and dress casually?

She cleared her throat nervously and tried to smile, then gave up. Crossing swiftly to the visitor's chair, she dropped into it and stared at him.

"I've given your suggestion some thought," she began, wishing she could clear the sense of desperation that gripped her.

He nodded and sat, his eyes focused on her. "And?"

"I would like some more information. I think we need to discuss this further."

"Information such as?"

"How you expect such an alliance to work," she blurted out.

So much for the carefully rehearsed speech she'd practiced in the cab.

He leaned back in his chair, his gaze never leaving hers.

"I expect we'll get along fine. We have for five years."

"I meant, precisely how do you see this working? Would I keep my apartment? Visit your place when you wanted to hold a party or something? Move in with you right away?"

Share a bed? That she couldn't voice, not yet.

He shook his head.

"Our arrangement must appear to be a normal marriage in every regard, Gemma. We have to convince your government that this is real. The Immigration and Naturalization Service'll interview and question us. INS will want to inspect our living arrangements. You'll have to give up your place and move into mine. If you don't like my apartment, we can look for something together that would suit us both. It's imperative that we convince Immigration that this is a true and lasting marriage. I understand they frown on foreign nationals making marriages just for the sake of remaining in the United States."

"Which this would be."

"As long as we give the appearance of a normal marriage, I doubt there will be any challenges. In fact, your pregnancy could work strongly in my favor. No one would question a hurry-up wedding if the bride is already pregnant."

She nodded—especially if they didn't bother to name the

real father. She kept her personal life private. She cleared her throat, wishing she had typed up a list of questions. Her mind spun, but no coherent thoughts seemed to come through. At last she spoke.

"You said a normal marriage. Normal, how? Like cooking and cleaning the apartment and shopping?"

Like sleeping together, kissing, making love?

She longed to ask about every aspect, but shyness kept her tongue silent. She wasn't looking for normal in any sense. Her lesson had been hard-learned, but permanent.

"I don't need a cook or maid. I have a man now who looks after the apartment. I see no reason Hal wouldn't continue his duties just because you'll be living there."

She nodded. What else was there?

"I have some furniture that belonged to my parents," she said. "I'd like to bring that."

"Of course. It will be your home, so do with it what you will."

"And I have lots of friends. I don't want to change that because of a new husband."

Although, until yesterday, she had planned to cease her friendships except for a few very close ones. She hated the thought of everyone knowing the circumstances of her baby.

"I wouldn't expect you to change your life drastically. My home would become your home. You'd be free to invite whomever you wished to visit us."

"I'm not good at social chitchat," she said, her mind still spinning.

He countered her every worry. Was she seriously considering the proposal?

A hint of amusement crept into Nikos' eyes.

"Neither am I, truth be told. I much prefer the working environment. But duty necessitates social obligations. Especially when dealing with business rivals, clients and vendors. It makes the entire process run more smoothly. You'll do fine, Gemma. You're polished and sophisticated...."

His voice trailed off as he glanced at her worn jeans.

She grimaced. "Fooled you, Nikos. This is me when I'm not working. I'm not into fancy dresses and lots of jewelry. I prefer jeans and comfortable tops. I'm not all that sophisticated or polished even after five years in New York. I clean up good. But my jeans are already getting tight. And in another few months, I'll be pretty big."

And on her best days, she never looked like a supermodel.

"I like what you're wearing," he said.

"You do?"

He astonished her.

"You hide your body in the business suits you normally wear. Now its shape's revealed. And a very nice sexy body it is, too. Very appealing."

She froze. The last thing she wished was to appear appealing. She wanted no attraction between them. This proposed marriage was for expediency only—nothing more. Color flushed her cheeks, and Gemma dropped her gaze to the polished surface of his desk. Tingling sensations skipped along her nerves. He'd never given a hint he'd noticed her as a woman. She was his personal assistant—being married wouldn't change that.

"You're a lovely woman, Gemma. I believe that we'll suit each other well or I would not have made the offer. Pregnant women usually seem quite beautiful. And we can afford to get the latest in haute couture for any stage of pregnancy. Have I answered your concerns? Is there anything else?"

"Sex," she blurted out before she could think.

"Ah. For or against?"

He didn't seem the least bit perturbed.

She glared at him. How dare he be so casual? Was he teasing?

Blood thundered through her veins again, heating her body. Making love with Nikos? Casual sex was never her thing. She'd thought herself in love with James—only to discover how false that proved. She could never sleep with a man who viewed her as part of a business deal. Did Nikos wish to make this temporary marriage normal in every respect?

She needed to know before making a final decision.

Definite amusement lurked in his eyes, which surprised her. She hadn't expected that. Gemma wished she could come up with a scathing putdown that would erase that mocking glint and restore her to an equal footing. But she could only feel the tumultuous emotions that threatened to overwhelm her.

"Perhaps that is a topic we could discuss at some length later," he said smoothly when she didn't answer.

"I would keep my job?" she asked, glad to change the subject.

"Of course. You're the best personal assistant I've ever had. As I told you, one reason I proposed this plan was to keep from losing you."

"Okay, then, I guess I'll marry you."

Nikos actually laughed.

"You're good for keeping a man's ego in line. I bet condemned prisoners sound more enthusiastic. But thank you. I'll endeavor to make sure you never regret your kindness."

"Um, I'll guess we'll see as time goes on, won't we?"

She rose. "Bye."

"Where are you going?"

"Today's Saturday. Unlike you, I don't plan to spend it at work. I have places to go and things to do."

"Such as?"

He rose and moved around the desk in that lithe grace she suddenly found fascinating.

Don't come any closer, she thought, panicking, *or I'll lose my train of thought.* But he obviously couldn't read minds, because he stepped right up beside her.

Gemma breathed in the scent of his aftershave. Spicy and masculine, it called forth a small fire deep within. What was wrong with her? She'd been closer to him many times and never had this reaction before.

"Um…"

She looked away and tried to think of some activity that would satisfy his curiosity.

When Nikos reached out to brush an errant strand of hair from her cheek, she jumped. Her gaze flying to his, Gemma held her breath. In all the years she'd worked for him, he'd never touched her.

And a good thing, too. Shimmering excitement danced along her cheek as the feel of his warm fingertips lingered. She searched his eyes for any sign he'd felt something when he touched her.

His oblique gaze revealed nothing. Impassivity was fine when dealing with longshoremen, but Gemma would have liked some sign of what Nikos was feeling. Was she the only one to notice that spark?

"If you have prior obligations, then do not let me detain you," he said. "Thank you for agreeing to become my wife. We will see to the arrangements on Monday."

Nikos reached for her hand and clasped it lightly in his, then lifted it and turned it palm up. Lightly he brushed his lips across her wrist.

"You do me honor in your agreement," he said in his husky voice with the slight British intonation.

"It is I who am honored," Gemma replied, still feeling the warmth his light caress engendered. "I'll make sure my baby does nothing to sully your family name."

He smiled slightly and leaned closer.

Pulling her hand free, Gemma turned and fled. She snatched up her purse in passing and hurried to the elevator. The car she'd come up in was still on the floor, so she instantly stepped inside and punched the button for the lobby, leaning against the side wall, willing the doors to close swiftly.

She tried to get her roiling emotions under control. She was engaged to Nikos Petropoulos. And he'd sealed their bargain with a kiss.

Not on the mouth, as she might have expected, but a kiss. One she could still feel. If she hadn't run like a scared rabbit, would he have given her an actual kiss?

Gemma turned right from the building entrance and began walking briskly to escape her thoughts. She couldn't believe she'd just agreed to marry the man. She still had a dozen questions, a dozen concerns. But it was too late—she'd said yes.

With an odd sense of elation, Nikos watched Gemma practically run from the office and head for the elevators. Slowly, he turned and moved to the windows. It was sunny and warm outside, but the climate control of the building gave little hint of the balmy weather. He wondered where Gemma was heading in such a hurry. The offices were too high for him to see her when she emerged from the building, but he watched the pedestrians, anyway.

He knew little about his assistant beyond how well she worked for him. Who were her friends? How had she gotten mixed up with a married man? Judging by the signs, she was hurt, afraid, and doubly wary now.

Which suited him. Their marriage was a business deal. When the crises had passed, they could each resume their normal lives. He didn't want her imagining she was falling in love.

From this moment on, however, she was his— temporarily.

A peculiar feeling of completion filled him. Her visit surprised him this morning, and he felt intrigued by her wearing clothes that were so different from the attire she usually wore to work. He liked her top. Its snug fit displayed her figure to full advantage. She was stunning.

The softness of her skin had been another surprise. Had she not pulled away so abruptly, he'd have kissed her again, moving this time to that inviting mouth that seemed to cry for his attention this morning.

How could he have overlooked it in the past?

Would she be shy in her kisses? Or daring?

Impatient with his thoughts, he turned back to his desk.

There were a few more items he wished to cover today. Monday, he'd have Elise clear his calendar for the week, except for the longshoreman's contract negotiations, which wouldn't wait. He wanted to be prepared for every demand and be able to back up his counteroffers with as much data as possible.

But just before he pulled the analyses from the folder, he looked through the door to where Gemma usually sat. He almost wished he'd been going with her today—wherever she was going.

Time enough when they were married to do things together. They hadn't discussed that possibility. He looked forward to Gemma's reaction when he brought it up.

When Gemma stepped off the elevator Monday morning, fellow workers wishing her well instantly surrounded her. Nikos had obviously wasted no time in letting the entire firm know about their pending nuptials.

"Thank you."

She smiled politely as two secretaries wished her happiness, then bombarded her with questions.

"So, tell us how it happened?"

"When did he propose?"

"Isn't he the most romantic man you know?"

"Where are you going to live?"

"Will you keep your job?"

Gemma looked at Monique. The young woman had worked for them for seven months. She was competent, but not at all satisfied with her job. Ambitious, she had yet to prove herself ready for additional responsibility. Sometimes Gemma thought the woman just wanted more money.

"Did you get your ring yet?"

With a glance of disappointment, Shelly looked at her left hand, then brightened. "Oh, I know, you'll shop for it together."

"Not likely," Monique interrupted. "I'm sure Nikos has a fortune in jewels in the family vault." She waved her hand vaguely. "He probably sent for them to present to his future wife. I imagine they're worth a small fortune. Won't you be worried wearing thousands of dollars' worth of jewels around here?"

Gemma shook her head, slowly making her way toward her office. She needed to speak to Nikos. Smiling, she tried to appear the happy fiancée and answer all their questions. The last thing either she or Nikos wanted was suspicions.

"I know nothing about jewels. We'll get things sorted out soon, and I'll let you all know. In the meantime, I have work to do, and I suspect you all do, as well. Excuse me."

Elise smiled sympathetically when Gemma reached her desk.

"Sorry, I think that ambush was my fault. When Nikos told me, I was so surprised and delighted that I called Betty in personnel. She is a bit of a blabbermouth."

Gemma rolled her eyes and nodded.

"You've got that right. Please, tell everyone I really appreciate their interest, but we have work to do."

"Including my new assignment, find out all I can about instant marriages in New York. If I can't get the answer soon, Nikos' threatening to fly out to Las Vegas tomorrow and marry you there."

"Great, just what I always wanted, a wedding with an Elvis impersonator officiating. Not."

Gemma crossed the room to her desk and wondered what it would be like to be so wildly in love with a man they were both impatient to get married.

Like she thought she and James might have been several months ago. In such an event, maybe even an Elvis wedding at some tacky chapel in Las Vegas would be worth it.

But this marriage was a business deal, one Nikos was obviously planning to complete as soon as possible to stall the INS. A quiet ceremony at City Hall would be much more his style.

For a moment, Gemma gave a thought to a traditional wedding. Since her mom had died in a plane crash when she was fourteen, Gemma had never really planned on a formal traditional wedding. She wondered if her father had once longed to walk her down the aisle. If her mother had wanted Gemma to wear her wedding dress. Had they not died, Gemma probably would still live in Ohio and would never have met Nikos. Or James.

If she and James had married, maybe she would have opted for a formal ceremony in memory of her parents. But Nikos' family didn't live in America, and she suspected he was not inviting them.

In fact, she wondered if he'd even tell them. There was no need. The marriage would be over in a few short months—and it wasn't as if it was real.

"Good morning, Gemma," Nikos said, coming out of his office. "I expect Frank LeBec to arrive in about ten minutes. We'll be reviewing some demands from the union. I have Phil and Josh joining us, and I want you to sit in on the meeting as well. Elise has the conference room set up. Anything you think I should know about LeBec? You've met him before—I haven't."

"He's a bit belligerent because of his lack of formal education, I've always thought. He had to drop out of school to help his family when he was a teenager, and as he moves up the ranks in the union, I think it bothers him more and more. He's fiercely loyal to his union and the men he represents. He'd rather do right by them than negotiate or be conciliatory," she said evenly.

Her voice didn't reflect the turmoil that had arisen unexpectedly upon seeing Nikos. She had better get used to it. She'd be seeing a lot more of him when they married.

His dark eyes had scarcely looked at her; he was reading the union's list of demands. Demands in addition to the normal scope of their latest contract.

Now he glanced at her.

"I asked Elise to find out about getting married."

"I heard. I met half the office staff when I got off the elevator. Our wedding is a seven-day wonder, and curiosity is rampant."

"What?"

Gemma smiled sweetly, though she longed to stamp her foot. What had he been thinking? Probably hadn't given the repercussions a thought.

"News travels fast and everyone wants to know what we are doing. I understand we might even make a quick stop in Las Vegas for the ceremony."

He frowned.

"I mentioned that in passing. I have no intention of flying to Vegas. We can get married here in New York. Elise will have all the information by the time we're finished with LeBec. No one said anything to me."

"Like they're going to question the big boss?"

He stepped closer. "But they harassed you?"

"It's not harassment. Friendly curiosity and open season for gossip. Some women who work here find you vastly romantic and think our marriage is a continuation of that romantic streak in you."

At least she'd be spared some of the speculation about her pregnancy when it became known—she hoped. She should be grateful for that. But she was still not feeling too charitable toward men. And it wasn't as if Nikos wasn't getting what he wanted from the deal.

"Romantic? That's nonsense."

"Oh, I don't know. I can see their point."

He stepped closer. Gemma felt the air leave the room. She would have stepped back, gained some space, but she was already against her desk. If she didn't want to duck to one side like a gawky schoolgirl, she had to hold her ground.

A deep breath—and she became conscious of Nikos' unique scent, masculine and entirely too tantalizing. Gemma longed for a moment's respite.

"You see their point? Maybe you could elaborate."

His voice was low, husky. Instantly Gemma imagined dark velvet-warm nights, Nikos with a woman alone in a quiet place, talking, touching…

Her imagination soared out of control. Swallowing, she tried to find the words to make the man step back. But nothing came to mind except how she'd like to feel his lips on her own.

Why did she keep thinking about a kiss? She'd sworn off men.

"Gemma?"

She cleared her throat.

"You are, um, rather, ah, exotic?"

"Exotic?"

"In a thrilling sort of way," she added rapidly, totally confused by the emotions that clamored within. Was this some kind of hormone-induced fantasy? Was she losing her mind?

"Thrilling? You intrigue me. Please continue."

How did she get into this? Where was Frank LeBec? Wasn't he supposed to be here by now?

"Well, you're wildly attractive, tall, dark, and handsome. Women notice things like that. And you're successful and rich and sophisticated and Greek men are known to be romantic."

He leaned even closer until Gemma could feel the puff of his breath caress her cheeks. Mesmerized by his dark eyes, she couldn't continue. Could scarcely put two thoughts together. Her entire body seemed to be tuned to his, yearned for his, wished to explore that mouth that was so temptingly near. She longed to brush her fingers through that dark hair; test the strength of his muscles. Feel his heat envelop her.

"I'm fascinated by this discussion. Please continue," he said.

His voice was like mulled wine—spicy and hot and intoxicating. Gemma wanted him to speak, not her—so she could listen to his voice and float away on the myriad feelings that tumbled inside.

She leaned back over her desk, trying for some distance, some perspective.

"Nikos, you're crowding me."

"You've intrigued me, Gemma. I'm interested to see if you feel as these other women do. If you find me exotic, fascinating, attractive."

His mouth was mere inches from hers. Gemma wondered what he'd do if she just leaned forward until her lips touched his. Before she could gather enough wits to respond, however, he straightened and stepped back.

"Much as I'd like to continue this right now, I hear Elise approaching. Frank LeBec must be here."

He moved to the door.

Gemma remained rooted to the spot. If she didn't have the support of the desk behind her, she'd have sunk to the floor. Taking a deep breath, she desperately sought control. She had a meeting to attend. No time to get starry-eyed about her boss or start imagining an attraction that wasn't there.

If his presence at work drove her wild, what would being married feel like? It was necessary for her to maintain control. She dared not imagine there was more to this relationship than was actually between them.

She'd set herself up for heartbreak once.

"Forewarned is forearmed," she muttered as she turned to get her notebook and a couple of pens.

Chapter Three

G emma knew she'd never make it through the day without going crazy. The meeting with Frank LeBec ended on a low note from her point of view. She hadn't been so inattentive in a meeting since she first started and feared she would make a mistake.

Yet how could she focus on business when her thoughts spun around her forthcoming marriage to Nikos?

Would they find common interests or live parallel but separate lives? Did he plan to remain in the States his entire life, or did he expect to return to his own country at some point in the future when he turned over the reins of the shipping line to a younger family member?

And always at the back of her mind hovered the question of what he expected from their marriage.

What did *she* expect?

At the conclusion of the meeting, she almost ran to her desk, hoping for a few minutes to herself. She ordered lunch from a nearby deli. She knew it reflected cowardice, but it also meant she could avoid her inquisitive co-workers for a while.

If she stayed late tonight, she could avoid them all together.

Gemma had finished the last of her sandwich when Nikos walked calmly into her office. He eyed the deli wrapping paper with distaste.

"If you are free for dinner this evening, shall we have it at my home? It will give you an opportunity to see the place and provide us with the time to speak privately about our plans."

Gemma nodded, wadding up the wrapping paper and tossing it into the trash.

"You'll have to give me directions."

She knew his apartment was on the west side of Central Park, but didn't know exactly where.

"No need, you'll be with me. Elise has discovered what we need to do to get a license. We'll leave this afternoon in time to arrive at City Hall before they close. After we acquire the license, there is a one-day waiting period before we can conduct the ceremony. Wednesday afternoon has been cleared. We'll be married then. Elise also located a moving company, which will pick up your furniture on Friday. If you'd prefer to be home on Friday when they arrive, we can work around that. Or I can have Hal handle it."

"What?"

Gemma stared at him.

"Did you not hear me?"

Gemma stood, unable to decide if she should laugh or shout. A hint of temper simmered. She leaned over her desk slightly, eyes narrowed.

"Let me understand this, Nikos. You've single-handedly arranged our entire wedding without consulting me? Arranged to move my stuff without even asking what I want to do?"

He nodded. "I need you to work on these negotiations, not become sidetracked with plans someone else can handle. I delegated the tasks to Elise, and she completed them."

"So we marry on Wednesday. Did it ever occur to you that I might wish to have some friends attend my nuptials? Or that maybe I have something already planned for Wednesday afternoon?"

Her voice rose on the last part, and Gemma took a deep breath.

It was nerves, nothing more.

But the man was so arrogant sometimes she could hardly stand it.

"Do you?" he asked calmly.

Tilting her chin, she met his gaze.

"What time? I'll check my calendar."

"Don't be foolish, Gemma. I already had Elise verify that you'd be free. We agreed to marry as quickly as possible. Wednesday isn't a busy day. Elise has canceled all appointments except those directly involved with the negotiations. When would be a better time?"

"That's not the point."

"Ah, maybe I'm missing something in this discussion."

Using the word "discussion" by him reminded her of their earlier "discussion." For a moment she became sidetracked. But she quickly recovered.

"I need to get something to wear," she said, stalling.

He looked at the royal-blue silk blouse she wore with a mid-calf-length black skirt.

"What you have on is lovely."

"Nikos, I am not getting married in black."

"Ah, I see there are subtle nuances to this marriage business."

She eyed him suspiciously. Was he mocking her? His bland expression gave nothing away. He'd been married before. He knew what was involved.

She wouldn't wear white, not four months pregnant. But a nice cream-colored suit would work. If she could find one.

"In America, brides do not get married wearing black," she said.

"Nor do they in my country."

Gemma hesitated. "I know very little about Greece. Is it lovely?"

He laughed softly, his teeth startling white against his tanned face.

"It's quite lovely, Gemma. My family's home is on the edge of the Ionian Sea. The tangy scent of salt water mingles with the fragrance of jasmine when we're in the garden. It's wonderful to walk along the shore in the moonlight. Away from the sea, the land becomes more arid. Yet it holds its own beauty. It's hot during the day, but cools off at night."

Excitement filled Gemma as she listened to Nikos describe his home. His voice took on a lyrical quality as he painted word pictures. She wistfully wished she could see it, experience it. It sounded romantic and mystical. Very unlike Ohio, and totally unlike New York.

"We must leave by four to accomplish everything. Tonight, you can tell me about your parents and your childhood. You have never mentioned them before. Are they happy memories?" Nikos said in a brusque tone.

"Before this, we had a working relationship. I don't mix work with personal."

"Indeed, you're a very private person, Gemma. I look forward to learning more about you in the weeks to come."

"I could say the same thing, Nikos. I imagine I'll be pretty easy to know, but I'm not so sure about you."

Nikos studied her thoughtfully for a moment, then turned to enter his office. Gemma was quite unlike Katrina. His personal assistant seemed almost fragile in comparison. His first wife had been wild and beautiful, demanding and restless. She'd delighted in spending his money, buying clothes and furnishings and jewels like a child let loose in a candy shop.

He hadn't minded indulging her at first. It was only when he saw her true nature that he grew resentful of her love for his money. When he'd discovered she didn't care for him as much as for his assets, and one of his business rivals, he'd started divorce proceedings.

He'd known Gemma for five years—yet knew nothing beyond what she allowed. But he detected no wild extravagances in her life.

He wondered what the full story was with the man who'd fathered her baby. What was the private Gemma like? Had she been devastated when the truth became known? For a moment he wondered if she'd have continued the relationship had there not been a baby.

No, not once she'd discovered the man was married. She was nothing like Katrina.

In more ways than one.

He thought about the jeans and the snug-fitting top she'd worn on Saturday. His first wife would not have been caught dead in such an outfit. Smiling slightly, Nikos knew he couldn't wait to see Gemma wear it again.

Crossing to his wide window, he gazed out over the busy city street without seeing a thing. He'd wanted to kiss her that morning. The softness of her lips beguiled him, the warmth and suspected sweetness of her mouth tantalized. As did the feelings that still gripped him.

He'd proposed this union to satisfy the INS. Now it looked as if he might get more from it than he expected.

Would Gemma have kissed him back?

Would she in the future?

How far did they dare take this marriage and be able to break apart in a few months?

Would she want to share a bed?

Did he want her there?

He needed to understand her better before pushing for more. But with the sanctity of marriage between them, they could enjoy each other, with no expectations to come crashing down later.

Except for the baby.

What did he know about babies? They were innocent creatures, not deserving of some things fate had in store for them. Still, he could make sure it had a good start in the world.

For a moment he wondered if it would be a girl or boy. Would the child look like Gemma? He could see a little chubby toddler with Gemma's chestnut hair and wide gray eyes running around. Where would he be when the baby was two? Would they continue their arranged marriage or have long since parted?

"Are you ready?" Elise asked when she phoned shortly before four o'clock.

"As I'll ever be," Gemma replied.

Quickly she straightened her desk, locking the sensitive folders in her drawer and stacking the rest of the papers. She slipped out to the ladies' room for a moment.

Checking to make sure her hair was neat, she studied herself in the mirror. She didn't look at all ruffled, yet inside, her stomach churned. She couldn't believe she'd agreed to this marriage. Was she crazy?

She took a deep breath and raised her chin. For better or worse, she was committed. It was just temporary. A solution to both their problems.

Nikos waited for her in her office. He let his gaze run across her lightly, then took her arm. "Ready?" he asked.

"Yes."

Gemma felt his touch tingling in every cell. She had difficulty remembering he was her boss. Her clamoring senses wanted to deny that relationship and seek another.

Instantly, the memory of his lips against her skin flashed into mind. Her wrist felt warm where he'd touched her. Licking her lips, she slid a glance sideways, almost feeling that kiss against her wrist. Would he kiss her on the mouth next time?

Her heart skipped a beat. She wasn't sure she could handle Nikos. Yet the vague yearnings around him made little sense. Would she prove a satisfactory wife for him, even temporarily?

Or would he end up regretting his hasty decision before the situation was resolved?

"Nikos?" she said when they were in the elevator. Amazing—they were alone.

"Yes?"

"If this doesn't work—"

"Why wouldn't it work?" he interrupted.

"I don't know, but I'm not sure I can pull it off."

"Pull what off?"

"Act like a wife for you."

"Let me be the judge of that, Gemma."

The car stopped at another floor, and three men entered.

Unwilling to pursue the conversation with others eavesdropping, Gemma fell silent.

Nikos flagged a cab with ease, handing her in and then climbing in beside her. Gemma moved closer to the far door, but Nikos' legs sprawled in the space, his knee touching hers. It was as if there was a direct link between them.

Staring out the window, Gemma saw nothing. While staring out the window, Gemma's entire body concentrated on Nikos and the spot where they touched.

It was distracting. She should think about their marriage, making sure she knew what she was doing. Instead, she could only fixate on that connection with Nikos and the roiling sensations that swamped her.

The cab ride to City Hall took longer than expected. Or had it only seemed endless? Gemma wasn't sure.

In contrast to the ride, getting the marriage license seemed to take only seconds. And they were soon back in another cab and headed for Nikos' apartment.

Gemma was curious to see it. She wondered if there'd be

room for any of her furniture. Would it blend in with his? Did he have very modern pieces and art she'd never understand?

He certainly was unlikely to have Early American furnishings, which she loved. Maybe she'd put her things in storage for a few months. Or maybe leave them where they were. She could continue to pay her portion of the rent and move back in with Susan after the marriage ended.

When the cab stopped before the tall stone building, Gemma realized the building sat directly across from Central Park. Did his apartment overlook the park? How nice to be so close to green space.

Gemma's spirits rose.

"Remember, Gemma, you may change things as you see fit. This will be your home," Nikos said as they ascended in the quiet elevator. The lobby had been small, but elegantly appointed.

Nikos had introduced her to the doorman, telling him of their planned wedding and Gemma's forthcoming move into the building.

Gemma felt as if she had stepped into a dream.

The soft chime of the elevator and the doors sliding open brought her back to reality. Nikos used a key and opened the door to his apartment, standing aside for her to enter.

Stepping inside, Gemma paused for a moment to take in the surroundings. They had stepped into a small foyer, with a long hall branching off to the left and right. Moving farther into the apartment, she entered the spacious living room. The wall opposite seemed to be made entirely of glass and overlooked the park.

For a moment she felt as if the room opened out and became a part of the outdoors. There were no curtains cutting into the view, no shades to block the light. Just a wide expanse of glass to admit the beauty of the park.

"Nikos, this is amazing."

The room itself reminded her of how she thought billionaires lived.

Thick Persian carpets covered the floor. Her heels sank into them. Without thinking, Gemma slipped out of her shoes and felt the lush carpets beneath her feet.

The furnishings defied categorizing. Traditional sofas faced the wall, with wing chairs flanking offering places to sit and enjoy the view. The room felt spacious, open, and comfortable.

Her expectation of sophistication evaporated. And she loved it.

"I'm pleased you like it, Gemma," Nikos said quietly, studying her as she absorbed the beauty of her surroundings.

She turned to discover he was standing beside her, his head inclined as he looked into her eyes.

"If you wish to change anything, you may," he said.

"I don't think I'd want to. It's totally unexpected, but fantastic."

Her toes curled into the carpet as she tried to think of something else to say. To think up a reason to step away from the spell that held her captive. Nikos stood so close she could reach out and touch him without moving but a few inches. His dark eyes seemed to look right down into her soul.

Shyly, she smiled.

"It reminds me of an English country home."

He nodded, and she felt her heart skip another beat.

Warmth filled her at his look. She felt almost light-headed.

The back of his fingers caressed her cheek, his fingers stopping beneath her chin, tilting her head to better gaze into her eyes.

"Good. Katrina had the room entirely filled with modern furniture and dozens of knickknacks. It was too much. I find simplicity soothing, and beauty in the handiwork of God from the park."

"At night, what do you see?"

"We are high enough to be assured privacy. The sparkling lights from the buildings in the distance are enchanting. You'll love it at night, as well. Ah, Hal."

Nikos lowered his hand and turned to greet the man who had silently stepped through the doorway.

"Gemma, this is Hal. Hal, your new mistress, Gemma Green, soon to be my wife. She and I will be married on Wednesday and she'll move in immediately."

"Welcome, madam."

Hal was a tall man, dressed in a traditional black trousers and a white shirt with a black tie. He reminded her of an English butler. She knew Nikos had attended Cambridge. Was that the reason for some of the English feel?

Nikos speech had a slight British intonation. Hal's was totally British.

"For the first few days, things will continue as always, Hal," Nikos instructed. "After Gemma's lived here awhile, she may wish to make changes. You'll be guided by her decisions."

"As you say." Hal nodded his head once to Nikos and once to Gemma.

"We'll have dinner at seven," Nikos said.

Hal nodded once more and quietly left the room.

"Come, I'll show you around the place," Nikos said, taking Gemma's arm in a gentle clasp.

The familiar sensations began spiraling through her body at his touch. She didn't understand it. She'd never felt this way around James or any other man.

Gratitude, that was it. Nikos was helping her beyond what she should have expected. It was no wonder she felt grateful to him.

By the time dinner was served, Gemma's head was spinning. The apartment consisted of twelve rooms. Nikos had shown her several bedrooms with en suite baths, a study and a formal dining room, besides an enormous kitchen.

The apartment was furnished with a variety of

furnishings—French provincial in one bedroom, modern chrome and glass in another and heavy Mediterranean in a third.

Nikos' bedroom looked very ordinary, which surprised Gemma. She wasn't sure what she'd expected. But the king-size bed with a rather plain oak headboard filled a good portion. A dark dresser and night stand complimented the bed.

"This room will be yours," Nikos said, opening an adjoining door.

The room was tastefully decorated in soft sea-green and bright yellow.

"You may wish to have your own furnishings in here. If so, Hal can take care of removing this furniture."

"This'll be fine. Actually, I thought I might leave my furniture in my apartment. Then when we end the marriage, I can move back with minimum effort."

"Impossible. I thought you understood we must make certain we provide an impression to the INS of being completely committed. No one must suspect the reasons for this marriage, nor that we do not plan to remain together forever. You need to move in here. We'll be a married couple sharing our lives."

"Oh, of course. I guess I didn't think it through," she murmured, annoyed with herself that she hadn't.

The INS would look into all aspects of their marriage with

a fine-tooth comb. And her keeping her apartment would be a blatant clue that all was not as it appeared.

And the INS also explained the reason for adjoining rooms. They had to look married—always. For a moment she wondered if she could go through with the charade, after all.

Nikos looked at her sharply. "Something wrong?"

"No, not at all."

She couldn't meet his eyes. Instead, Gemma studied the room as if her life depended upon being able to reconstruct it from memory. It was only for a few months. And she had her baby to think about.

"Gemma—" Nikos turned her to face him, his hands on her arms "—we have five bedrooms in this apartment. If this one doesn't suit, we can find another."

Yours?

Gemma blinked and desperately prayed she had not uttered the word aloud. Where had that thought come from?

She stepped back.

"No, really, Nikos, this is perfect. And we need to keep up the pretense of a normal marriage."

"Unless such a time arrives that you feel comfortable sharing my room, perhaps?"

He did read minds.

Mesmerized, she stood still, her eyes caught in his dark gaze, totally unable to form a single sound.

Share Nikos' room? His bed? Her heart thundered in

response to the images that danced in her imagination. Of his strong, sleek body pressed against hers, of his mouth kissing her as she had imagined only that morning. Escalating the spark of interest deep within until it raged as full-fledged desire. A conflagration only his touch could ignite and extinguish.

"You never thought of that?"

His voice splashed through her like mulled wine, intoxicating every sense with its melodious tone. His head blotted out the rest of the room when he brushed her lips with his. Gemma opened her mouth slightly and caught her breath.

"I'm not sure this is such a good idea," she whispered.

Her voice wouldn't obey her. She wanted to sound firm and assured; instead, she sounded breathless and uncertain.

"Ah, but we need to get to know each other better, right?" he said, his lips scant millimeters from hers.

He closed the distance and kissed her deeply.

Gemma felt as if she were floating as the room spun round. The only solid anchor in a world turned topsy-turvy was Nikos. Naturally, she clung to that anchor. Her hands gripped his shoulders, and she tilted her head slightly. Opening her mouth at his insistence, she felt the wonder of his kiss to her toes. Lost in the magic of his touch, she gave herself up to the sheer pleasure found in his arms.

When he pulled back, she was stunned at her reaction.

There was no place for such activity in a business arrangement. The sooner she made her position clear, the better. It was as if cold water had been dashed in her face. She stepped back, feeling almost bereft, but determined not to give in to temptation so easily in the future.

Was Nikos assessing how willing a bride he'd gained? Had the kiss meant anything to him?

Feeling lost, Gemma brushed her hands down her skirt and turned to head back to the living room. Theirs was not a love match—she knew that better than anyone. And she didn't wish it to be. She'd experienced enough heartache and disappointment. She had no intentions of going down that path again.

Nikos had proposed a business alliance, and that was what she'd agreed to. His kisses were extraordinary. But she'd remain aloof, untouched. She didn't trust him, nor any man.

But her blood still raced through her veins. Her heart still beat heavily from the excitement of his embrace. She could tell herself to ignore him all she wanted, but she wondered if her body would ever listen.

"Come on, we'll sit in the living room and talk until dinner," Nikos said.

Glancing at him as she passed, she was peeved to note he appeared totally unaffected by their kiss. Good.

At least she tried to tell herself that.

Hal had set the dinner table with beautiful china, elegant

silver and delicate crystal, Gemma noted when called to dinner some time later. The table looked fit for royalty.

Gemma sat at Nikos' right, doubts and uncertainty plaguing her.

"Do you dine like this every night?" she asked.

"No. Hal has outdone himself tonight for the special occasion of your first meal with us."

"It's lovely. I wasn't sure if I had to live up to this daily."

She should say something about the kiss, explain what she was willing to do for this marriage and what she was not willing to do, but the words wouldn't come.

"We'll have settings like this for special events or when we have guests over."

"Otherwise it's paper plates in the kitchen, huh?" she said, trying to lighten the atmosphere.

His gleam of amusement brought a strong sense of satisfaction to Gemma. Sometimes she wondered if she'd lose sight of who she was when she was with this man.

Time to reassert her own personality. If he planned to go through with this charade, it was time he knew what he was getting.

Hal entered, placing a bowl of soup before each of them.

"Perhaps not so casual. But the dishes we will normally use are not fine china. Do you like to cook, Gemma? Will you be vying for time in the kitchen with Hal?"

"No worry there. I like to bake brownies or cookies once

in a while, but I have done little cooking lately. It's hardly worth it for a single person."

"Ah, but what about friends? Do you entertain?"

"Rarely. We usually go out and each pay our own way. After working all day, the last thing I want to do is more work, and that's what I think cooking is. Though my mother was a great cook."

"Was she? Tell me about your parents, Gemma."

"My mom died when I was fourteen. My dad only a few weeks later. I thought he died of a broken heart. They were very close. I lived with an aunt until I moved here. Aunt Bea died just before I came to work for you. No other close family. Until my baby's born," she said briefly.

As the meal progressed, Gemma relaxed. The food was prime rib, twice-baked potatoes and a collection of steamed vegetables. Another case of Hal outdoing himself for her first dinner?

She didn't question it, just enjoyed every morsel.

"We'll take our coffee in the living room," Nikos said at the end of the meal.

"Thank you, Hal, it was perfect." Gemma said as she rose to join Nikos after they finished. "I'll skip the coffee, however. I'm not having caffeine these days."

"My pleasure, madam," Hal said formally.

"You've made his day," Nikos said a few minutes later as they sat on the sofa in the living room.

"Katrina never said thank you or told him that a meal was delicious."

Hal entered the living room and set a tray before them on the coffee table, fragrant coffee in a fragile pot. A second pot contained hot water. Two cups and a small plate of assorted tea bags completed the tray.

"I brought an assortment of herbal tea," he told her.

"Thank you. I appreciate that," Gemma said with a smile.

"Hal was here then?" Gemma asked as she poured a cup for Nikos after Hal had left. She was touched he'd brought her tea.

Did that show he approved of the forthcoming alliance? Or only that his training was excellent?

"Yes."

His clipped tone clued her in. He didn't want to discuss his ex-wife.

Then why had he brought up her name?

"Shall we discuss the wedding?" she asked.

"It will be the two of us and witnesses. Elise has scheduled it with a judge. Tomorrow you can find a suitable dress."

"So, will we leave work early or just dash out on our lunch break?"

She couldn't help the hint of impatience in her tone. Wasn't the bride supposed to have some say in her own wedding—no matter how arranged it was?

He glanced at her, raising one eyebrow.

"We will be married at one o'clock, eat a celebration luncheon and then return home."

"Here, you mean?"

"Of course. This is your home now, Gemma."

She didn't feel at home.

Time would change that. At least she hoped so.

Would it also change how she felt about Nikos?

Exactly how did she feel about this man?

Grateful he was willing to marry her. Intrigued by the personal glimpses she'd seen today. Fascinated by the attraction that seemed to grow every moment she spent with him.

But she wouldn't forget for an instant that this was a temporary arrangement. No more fairy-tale love stories for her. Once they separated, she'd be free to live her life just as she wished.

For an instant, Gemma wondered if that would be enough.

Chapter Four

Tuesday, Gemma found it hard to concentrate at work. She arrived early to avoid other employees. Try as she might, she couldn't concentrate on the tasks at hand, instead kept remembering the previous evening with Nikos.

Remembering and anticipating the next time the two of them were alone. Would he kiss her again? Touch her hand, brush back her hair? Looking up, she wished she could see behind closed doors.

When he'd arrived that morning, he'd gone straight to his office after a brusque hello and shut his door. She hadn't seen or heard from him since.

By noon, Gemma gave in. She couldn't do her job effectively. Instead, she'd go look for something to wear to her wedding.

Stopping at Elise's desk, she told her she was taking the rest of the day off.

"Nikos didn't mention that to me," Elise replied, checking her calendar.

"Yes, well, he should have. If he asks for me, tell him I'll see him tomorrow."

"At the wedding. I'm attending," the older woman said, her face wreathed in smiles.

"Good, I'll need all the friends there I can get."

Oops, that didn't sound like a blushing bride. Pretense was harder than she suspected.

Elise looked startled. "Why?"

With another look at Nikos' closed door, Gemma sighed, trying to come up with a reason for her comment that would satisfy Elise.

"You know how forceful he can be. It's hard to hold my own sometimes."

Like with the wedding arrangements he'd made without a by-your-leave. Eyes narrowed, she glared at his door. Their marriage was for mutual convenience. She was bringing him something he couldn't get on his own, just as he was helping her out of a very awkward situation.

"I think being swept off my feet by such a handsome man would be thrilling," Elise said, smiling.

Gemma turned her gaze to the older woman and noted the dreamy expression. Even Elise felt the magnetism. How was she supposed to resist if she was living with the man? Remembering the charade, Gemma forced a smile.

"It is thrilling. He's wonderful. I think I have pre-wedding jitters."

"That's common. Don't worry about it, they'll pass. When

Joe and I married, I was a nervous wreck for weeks before the event. We had a big church wedding and—"

Elise stopped abruptly. "I guess it was different for us."

Gemma nodded.

"This will suit us both fine. I don't have any family. My friend Susan will be my bridesmaid tomorrow. I thought about inviting a few other friends, but decided we can have a reception later and invite everyone."

Or not, since the marriage probably wouldn't last long enough to bother with such festivities. But no need to tell Elise that.

"Anyway," Gemma continued, "if he asks, tell him I've gone to get my wedding dress."

After stopping at a nearby deli for lunch, Gemma then caught a cab to one of Manhattan's trendiest boutiques. She'd heard of the place for years and never considered entering it, much less buying something from it.

However, if her only wedding wasn't a time to splurge, Gemma didn't know what would be.

The boutique was spacious and quiet, despite the many women shopping. A smartly tailored young woman came up to her only seconds after she entered. Within an hour, Gemma had the perfect silk suit and darling veiled hat. Matching accessories took only a little longer, and by late afternoon she was on her way home. Extremely pleased with her selection, she hoped Nikos would appreciate how nice she looked.

Susan was still at work, so Gemma had the apartment to herself. Changing into jeans, she began to sort and pack some things she'd take to Nikos' apartment. Marking those items she wanted, she wondered if Susan would want the things she didn't care to move.

The phone rang.

"Hello?"

"Are you all right?"

Nikos' strong voice came across clearly.

"Sure. Why?"

"Elise said you left before lunch."

"And did she tell you why?"

He paused a moment. "No."

"Did you give her a chance to?"

"I looked for you and when I didn't see you, I asked her. She said you'd left for the day. Then I tried your cell. There was no answer."

"I went shopping."

The silence stretched out for several seconds.

"Shopping?"

"For a wedding dress. Remember, according to your very complete plan, Tuesday was the day to shop for a wedding dress."

"Ah yes, because black wouldn't suit."

"Right."

"So, did you get one?"

"Yes, and it's definitely not black."

"White?"

"Sort of off-white. And a little hat with a veil."

Did he care at all, or was she babbling to cover the nervousness that crept up? Sitting beside the phone, Gemma took a deep breath. This was just Nikos, her boss for five years.

And the man who had kissed her last night. A kiss like none other.

"So you will be the epitome of a traditional bride."

"Maybe not the epitome, but fairly traditional. Is that a problem?"

"Not at all. I look forward to seeing you in the morning. Shall I pick you up at noon?"

"You can't pick me up. It's bad luck to see the bride before the ceremony. Susan and I will get a cab and meet you at the judge's chambers."

"I'll send Hal. He can drive you. And you can give him your bags. He'll bring them back to the apartment so they'll be waiting for you here when we return. I've had Elise book us for lunch at the Waldorf. I'll make sure she includes Susan."

"Who else is coming?" Gemma asked, again a bit annoyed he was arranging things without asking her opinion.

Strong-willed and forceful as he might be, she would not let everything go his way.

"Elise, Phil Mannering and Abe Miller." Although Gemma had never met Abe, she knew he and Nikos had been friends for many years.

"Not your cousin Allessandros?"

The pause was barely discernible.

"I haven't yet informed my family of our marriage."

"I see."

But she didn't. Was it some big, dark secret? Was he hoping to marry, get his green card and discard his new wife before his family learned of their nuptials?

"I doubt it, but I don't have time to go into that now. I'll see you tomorrow."

"Nikos, what did you want? Why were you trying to get me at the office?"

"I wanted the updated numbers on that new freighter in the Pacific, the *Alabaster*."

"Those figures are in the left drawer, about three folders down. Elise can get them for you."

"I'm not so helpless I can't get them myself," he returned dryly.

Nikos hung up the phone. He'd used that as an excuse to call her. When he'd discovered she'd left for the day, he'd immediately wondered if something was wrong. He knew little about pregnant women, only that they could suffer from morning sickness and other problems.

And for a split second, he wondered if she was having regrets about agreeing to their upcoming marriage. Her buying the dress should reassure him. But it didn't.

He leaned back in his chair and turned to gaze out over Manhattan. It was unlike him to worry about what others did or thought. It had been a long time since he moved beyond that. He considered the solution he'd proposed perfect for them both. He'd keep his personal assistant and give her the help she needed.

And he'd get his visa extended—permanently.

But was there more?

For a moment, he let himself recall the kiss they'd shared last night. Gemma had been sweet, shy and surprised. He felt it all. She could keep an impassive demeanor while working, but her emotions were clear to him last night.

And the pull of attraction surprised him.

He'd dated before and after his brief marriage. Beautiful women, sophisticated, talented, articulate. Some he desired, many he did not. But none touched his sense of protectiveness, like Gemma. None raised questions that could only be answered by getting to know her better.

For having worked with her for five years, he really knew only the most superficial information about his assistant. Soon to be his wife.

He looked forward to discovering more aspects of her as they lived together.

And maybe explore that potent attraction.

Hal picked up Gemma and Susan the next day and delivered

them to the courthouse. As they walked into the marble-floored lobby, Gemma felt almost sick. She knew it wasn't from the pregnancy, but from sheer nerves. She hadn't slept well. Worry about the advisability of taking this step plagued her.

"Are you okay?" Susan asked.

They had been roommates for the five years Gemma had worked at ALK Shipping and had developed a strong and lasting friendship.

Susan was short, a bit plump, and the best friend Gemma had ever had.

"You look a bit green around the gills."

"Great, I hope the color goes well with my suit."

"You look fine, just a bit off color. Having doubts?"

Susan was the only person besides Gemma and Nikos who knew the entire story behind the wedding. "It's not too late to say no."

"And do what—move to California?"

"I've told you a dozen times no one pays that much attention to unmarried mothers these days."

"And I've told you back it would matter to me. Blame it on my small-town upbringing. Anyway, I'm committed. Just a bit nervous."

They found the judge's chambers and entered. Nikos was already there, standing near the window conversing with the judge. Phil and another man Gemma didn't recognize. Must be his friend Abe.

"Wow." Susan said. "Is that hunk by the window the groom? Tall, dark and devilishly handsome? If you don't fall madly in love with him, send him my way."

Gemma swallowed. The last thing she wanted to do was fall in love with anyone. Much less Nikos Petropoulos.

He looked up and saw her. Without a word to the men he'd been talking with, he crossed the room to her.

"Gemma."

He reached for her hand and kissed the palm, enclosing it in his own as he turned to Susan.

"You must be Susan."

"Yes, Susan Abernathy. I guess you're Nikos."

"I'm pleased Gemma has a good friend to join us today."

"I just hope this all works."

He raised an eyebrow and looked at Gemma.

"The marriage and all," she said. "Is everyone here? Are we ready to start?"

He pulled her slightly to one side and reached for a small florist box on the table.

"I took the chance the colors would suit," he said, offering her the box.

When Gemma opened it, she found a lovely corsage of pink roses and white baby's breath. Susan stepped up and helped her fasten it to her suit.

"Now you really look like a bride," her friend said, giving

her a hug.

Elise hurried in, and with the entire wedding party present, they were ready to start.

The judge began the familiar service and Gemma listened as if in a trance. The opening was nice and sounded just as if they were truly getting married. Which they were, she reminded herself. Just because it seemed like a dream didn't mean it wouldn't be legal and binding.

"Do you, Gemma, take Nikos to be your lawful wedded husband, to love, honor and obey, in sickness—"

Gemma became instantly alert.

"Wait."

The judge stopped. Nikos looked at her.

"Say that part again."

The judge began again, and as soon as he reached the word *obey*, Gemma stopped him.

"No." She turned to Nikos. "No 'obey' in the vows. I never agreed to that. I'm not some child to be directed by someone else."

"Gemma, it's just part of the ceremony."

"No."

With a suppressed sound of frustration, Nikos took her arm and walked her across the room, where they'd have a modicum of privacy.

"What's going on?" he asked, leaning close, his glare capturing Gemma.

"I will not promise to obey you unless you promise to obey me and say your part first. That's all. I didn't know he would use such an antiquated ceremony. I know the newer version doesn't say 'obey'."

"For goodness sakes, it's just a ceremony."

"And can you promise me in all the time we'll be married you will never say to me you must do it my way or you must obey me in this because you promised when we were married?"

He stared at her for endless moments.

"I wouldn't say that."

"I've worked with you for five years. I know how you operate. When you really want something, you go after it with everything you have. And this is just the perfect thing to add to your arsenal when making a point."

"I can't believe you've stopped everything over one word."

"Then eliminate the word or include it in your vows. Your choice."

He shook his head and looked around. The others were waiting near the judge, watching them curiously. Susan fought a smile. Abe seemed amused.

Looking back at Gemma, Nikos asked softly, "Are you going to be this difficult all the time?"

She smiled at him and shook her head. "Consider this our first compromise. And isn't that a big part of marriage?

Compromising, so we both come out ahead?"

"Fine."

He inclined his head once and then started back toward the judge.

Gemma didn't know if she could claim a victory or not. But at least she'd stood up for herself. She knew she had to make sure Nikos didn't overwhelm her.

After a brief conference with the judge, Nikos indicated he should continue, which he did—omitting "obey" from her vows.

"You may kiss the bride," the judge ended.

Nikos brushed a light kiss across her lips and turned to shake the judge's hand.

Gemma felt disappointed. She'd expected more. For a moment she thought she might cry. Was that it? A light brush of lips for the wedding kiss? The kiss in the apartment the other night had held more emotion, more passion.

"Congratulations. And best wishes." Susan hugged her.

Then Elise. Abe shook her hand, offering his best wishes.

"I brought a camera. Want some pictures with the judge?" Susan asked. "I'm your official wedding photographer."

"I brought my camera," Elise added. "Wouldn't be a wedding without pictures."

Gemma smiled, though she felt uncertain inside. Would Nikos stand for further nonsense about a wedding, or now that the deed was done, would he hasten back to work after lunch to have the legal department contact the INS?

He surprised her. When Susan told him what she wanted, he posed with Gemma, his arm around her waist, pulling her close to him. She could smell the scent of his aftershave, which brought memories of the night at his apartment.

The warmth of his hand against her waist spread. Her breathing caught and for a moment she felt light-headed. Her blood pounded through her veins and echoed in her ears.

Smiling, turning this way and that, she made it through the battery of pictures both Susan and Elise insisted upon. But she felt disjointed, out of control. Nikos Petropoulos was her husband. She was no longer Gemma Green, but Gemma Petropoulos.

Lunch was a blur. She hoped she talked coherently, but couldn't remember a single sentence.

Settled after lunch in the extravagant limousine Nikos had hired, Gemma suddenly longed for her freedom. She'd had it made when she was single. She could go where she wanted, do what she wanted.

Now she had agreed to a marriage to provide Nikos a way to remain in the U.S. and save her own pride when the pregnancy became obvious. She had to play her part of a loving devoted wife well to allay any suspicion of the INS— or the gossips at work.

Could she do that? Pretend to feel strongly for her husband while all the while trying to keep her distance? She couldn't let herself fall for him, as Susan had suggested. She already knew she wasn't his type. If a worldly beauty like Katrina couldn't hold him, how could a woman from a small town in Ohio?

"Tired?" Nikos asked as the limousine slid quietly through the Manhattan traffic.

"No. Still keyed up a bit."

"Despite your interruption, the ceremony went well. I liked it better than the elaborate affair Katrina dreamed up."

Ignoring the reference to his first wife, Gemma gazed out the window. They were heading uptown—toward his apartment. Their apartment.

"Are you planning to return to work today?" she asked.

"No. If we are to give the impression this is a genuine marriage, I don't see a doting husband deserting his wife on their wedding day."

"I guess not."

"In fact, I think we should take the rest of the week off."

She looked at him in surprise.

"While I like the idea, you need to work on your husband skills. You don't just announce things. We need to discuss them and decide mutually what we'll do."

His eyes danced with amusement.

"I see I have created a different person in Gemma, the wife from Gemma, the personal assistant."

"I start as I mean to go on," she said defensively.

"And for how long will we go on? I wonder," he said.

"What do you mean?"

"We agreed to marry for expediency. But I've been thinking that it might work out well enough to continue even after your baby is born and I have the green card. Unless, of course, you have other plans."

She shook her head. Had she heard him correctly? He'd be interested in continuing this marriage of convenience indefinitely?

"Only time will tell, I think," he said.

Hal greeted them when they arrived at the apartment.

"I've put your bags in your room, madam. If you wish for me to unpack, please tell me."

"No, that's all right, I can manage," Gemma said quickly. She needed something to keep her busy for the afternoon.

"Change into something you find comfortable and join me in the living room when you feel like it," Nikos suggested.

Gemma took her time changing and sorting and putting away her clothes. The closet was huge and her few skirts, business suits and dresses looked lost. The built-in shelves would hold twice as many clothes as she had brought.

She gazed at the view from her window. If she angled her head just right, she could get a view of Central Park. But the living room was the place to be for that view.

Wishing she didn't feel awkward and uneasy, she finally decided she couldn't remain in her room forever.

Wandering into the living room, she was disappointed to find she was alone. She thought Nikos would be waiting for her.

Hal appeared as if summoned.

"Would you like something to drink, madam?"

"Do you have any fruit juice?" she asked.

"Certainly. We have orange, apple, cranberry and grape."

"That's quite a selection. I'll have some cranberry juice."

He inclined his head.

"Nikos said you are expecting, so I made sure we have food and beverages that will be of healthy benefit."

Flustered, she nodded and watched as he almost glided from the room. It would take some getting used to having a butler. Especially one who seemed to know everything already.

No matter what Nikos said about seeing how long they might wish to continue their marriage, there were too many differences standing between them. The major one being status in life. She knew he was wealthy. But the difference between their lifestyles was becoming clear.

"I like that shirt on you."

Nikos stood in the opening from the hall.

Gemma turned and smiled, then felt her heart rate increase.

Nikos was wearing dark jeans and a blue polo shirt. The clothes emphasized his slim physique and displayed the muscular chest and arms.

He'd always looked wonderful in his tailored suits. Now he was breathtaking. Sexy and virile and overwhelmingly masculine.

Her fingertips itched to explore that broad chest, to touch him, feel his heat pour into her. Her heart sped up like she'd just run a race.

He came into the room, and her heart skipped a beat.

"Is Hal taking care of you?" he asked.

"He's bringing me some juice."

It was with monumental effort she raised her gaze to meet his eyes. Licking her suddenly dry lips, she cleared her throat.

"He knows I'm pregnant?"

"I told him. Just, as I guess from her comment, you told your roommate the truth about our marriage."

"Susan won't tell anyone."

"And if Immigration asks her questions?"

"Why would they?"

"If they suspect this marriage is false, they may question everyone who knows us."

"She starts her vacation this weekend. She's going to Mexico for an archaeological dig. Someone will surely decide by the time she gets back. She's my best friend. She'd have suspected something was weird when I went to work planning to give notice and returned engaged."

"Your powers of persuasion couldn't have convinced her you fell madly in love and agreed to my proposal for that purpose?"

She grinned.

"Nope. My powers of persuasion are not *that* strong" "

"And there is the baby's father. Do you miss him?"

Gemma shrugged and turned away, strolling over to the wide expanse of windows.

"I don't. I'm still angry more than anything when I think of him. If he truly loved me as he told me, why would he have let our relationship go so far without telling me the truth?"

"Perhaps he does love you and cannot get out of the marriage. I can see a man wanting to keep you—no matter what the cost."

Gemma spun around—to find Nikos right beside her. How had he crossed the room so silently?

His dark eyes gazed down at hers.

She turned the wedding band on her finger, uncertain how to take his comment.

"Are you flirting with me?"

"And if I am?"

Gemma smiled. "It seems odd."

She liked it too much. He might be comfortable flirting, but she must remember this was merely a temporary arrangement. She wasn't falling for another man to have that expectation fall through.

"Perhaps too soon. In the meantime, come and tell me some more about my new wife."

Sinking on the comfortable sofa cushions, Gemma

wondered how she'd ever get up again. But they felt wonderful. Looking out the window, she felt as if she were on top of the world.

"What do you want to know?" she asked.

"What you were like at age five."

"And if I tell you that, will you share with me?"

His childhood would fascinate her. About growing up in Greece. It sounded so faraway and so exotic.

"Of course, isn't that also a part of marriage—besides the compromises you spoke of?"

Hal brought juice for them both and quietly retired.

Hesitating only a moment, Gemma talked about her childhood in Elmsville, Ohio. Wondering how different it was from his, she told about her first bicycle, about starting school and about slumber parties.

She kept her gaze firmly fixed on the view of the park, and not on the sight of Nikos sprawled so casually beside her on the wide sofa, lest she become tongue-tied and forget what she wanted to say.

At one point, he reached out and unfastened her clip. Fingers combing through her hair, he gazed at her while she talked.

She stopped talking and looked at him, her eyes wide.

"Your hair has sunshine in it," he said whimsically. "And it's as soft as the finest silk. I couldn't resist touching it."

His fingers toyed with strands, as if memorizing the texture.

"I've seen it worn pulled back for five years. But never like this, soft and full around your face." He spoke as if talking to himself. "It suits you."

"It's easier to keep it pulled back at work," she said breathlessly.

"Ah, but more feminine like this."

Slowly, he leaned forward, and Gemma held her breath.

Chapter Five

Gemma's heart raced as she parted her lips. She knew she'd lost her mind. Instead of anticipating Nikos' kiss, she should jump up and put the length of the room between them.

In a minute.

First she wanted—

Hal cleared his throat.

Nikos slowly released the cascading waves of hair and sat back, looking impassively at his servant.

"Yes?"

"Excuse the intrusion, Mr. Mannering is calling. He says it's urgent."

Hal held out a cordless ivory phone.

Nikos took it and sat up.

"Yes?"

Gemma struggled to rise from the low divan. She ignored Hal and walked to the floor-to-ceiling windows to gaze sightlessly out on the springtime beauty of Central Park. She hugged herself as she tried to find some rational thought.

What was she doing letting herself be seduced by Nikos? Hadn't she learned enough from her experience with James to know that men had their own agenda?

It was easy for Susan to fantasize about Nikos; she didn't have to live with him or work with him. Or consider what their next step would be. Gemma did.

She needed to be very careful not to get caught up in the make-believe world they were creating. He valued her as an employee—this absurd idea of marriage proved that. Plus, she was able to help him out.

Nothing had changed. Unless he thought because they were married, he could now change that relationship.

"Gemma."

She turned. He'd laid the phone on the side table.

"What did Phil have to say?" she asked, keeping her distance.

They had to settle things before she'd feel comfortable again.

"He contacted Immigration. They are naturally suspicious, considering the haste of our wedding. We are to meet with an inspector the day after tomorrow. If he isn't satisfied with our explanation, the deportation will go forward."

"Then we have to make sure he's satisfied, don't we?"

"A single interview with us probably won't be the end."

Gemma shrugged. "We'll do the best we can."

"And as long as we present a united front to the world, he won't find anything amiss."

She eyed him suspiciously.

"What does a united front mean?"

Slowly, he smiled. Gemma felt her heart melt. Did he have a clue how devastating that smile was? How it made her feel tingly inside, as if her blood were filled with effervescent bubbles like fine champagne?

"To the world, we'll appear as a devoted couple. We'll start at the party Sven Johannsen is giving Friday night. He has a new artist as protégé and is hosting a showing at the gallery on Fifth Avenue."

"This Friday night?"

"Yes. I've already accepted the invitation. You'll attend with me, of course."

"You must have to have been sure you wouldn't be deported before then. Don't you think you could have asked me first?"

He rose with one easy move and walked across the room to her.

Or at least Gemma tried to think of it as walking, though it had the earmarks of a panther stalking his prey. Controlled, smooth, but focused and direct.

She swallowed hard.

Start as you mean to go on, she admonished herself.

"Nikos, if this is going to work at all, we have to come to

some kind of understanding. At work, you're the boss. What you say goes. But this isn't work. If you want me to consider this my home, then I get some say in things."

He nodded once, his attention focused on her.

Gemma took a deep breath.

"If you want to do things as a couple, then I need to be given the chance to take part in making plans."

"These plans were made before we even discussed our marriage."

"Then I don't need to go. They obviously were satisfied with you coming alone before. Nothing has to change."

"Don't be naïve. Can you imagine the rampant rumors if I show up two days after the wedding without my wife?"

Gemma tried to find a way to make him understand where she was coming from. She'd had years of practice dealing with his high-handed way of working. Surely she could find a satisfactory way to have a harmonious home life for however long the marriage lasted.

"Maybe I have other plans. Maybe—"

"Cancel them," he said ruthlessly.

She blinked.

"This will not work if you think you can order me around. This isn't the army, and you're not my commanding officer."

"Army? What are you talking about?"

"You. You're so used to ordering everything you don't even realize you're doing it. But not in a relationship with a woman. With me specifically."

"Do you have other plans?" he asked.

She shook her head.

"That's not the point. I might have. All I want is for you to see me as a person in my own right—to be asked."

He took a deep breath, running the fingers of one hand through his hair.

"Gemma, I have an invitation to a party at Sven Johannsen's on Friday night. Would you do me the honor of attending with me?"

She smiled and nodded. "I'd love to go."

He frowned. "Are you playing games?"

He stepped closer.

Gemma held her ground.

"No, just establishing ground rules, I guess."

"I don't remember having had a lot of complaints from other women I've taken out."

"Then they spoiled you. You've lived in America long enough to know women like to be independent."

"I've had no complaints from you over the last five years."

"What I put up with at work isn't the same as what I'm willing to put up with at home."

He reached out and brushed her hair back from one cheek, letting the back of his fingers caress her skin.

"Your skin is as soft as a baby's. And your hair is like hot silk."

"Are you deliberately changing the subject? I don't think we should do this."

Where was the decisive tone she needed? Her voice came out totally breathless.

"Ah, but don't you think a husband and wife are allowed a certain amount of, shall we say, intimacies?"

"But we're pretending."

"The feelings I'm experiencing right now don't feel like pretend."

Slowly, he drew her closer.

Gemma put up her hands to push him away. Only when her fingers touched his heat, she lost the will to push. She wanted to explore, to touch, to uncover every bit of the mystery surrounding her husband.

When he kissed her, she forgot even that quest. Parting her lips, she returned his kiss with rising passion. Caught up in the moment, she could only hang on while her senses soared. She delighted in the feel of his hard body against hers, in the pleasure that cascaded through her.

When he ended the kiss, he didn't pull away, but trailed nibbles along her cheek, to her neck and throat, kissing the wild pulse point at its base.

Gemma didn't know how her arms came to be holding him, or how her fingers became threaded through his thick hair, but she took advantage of the situation, exalting in the sensations that continued to sweep through her.

He wanted her. She was experienced enough to know that. For a moment she almost gave in to impulse.

But caution held her back. Had her slowly release her hold.

Nikos felt the change because the kisses became lighter until they were no more.

He rested his forehead on hers and gazed into her eyes.

"We're married. And I haven't lived like a monk. But we will do nothing to ruin this relationship. If you want to take it beyond the platonic, let me know. Otherwise..."

She nodded. She didn't know what she wanted. Right now she wanted to have more kisses, to feel his hands on her body, to know the soaring ecstasy she suspected only Nikos could give her.

But she didn't trust herself with men anymore. How did she know what the real agenda might be? After James...

No, she wasn't going there again. James was her past. Nikos was her present. She didn't know about the future.

But she was too unsure of anything right now to bank on any certainty.

Gently disengaging herself, she tried to smile. Knowing it was a futile effort, she stopped.

"I guess we need to see how it goes before taking any steps that might complicate things."

He straightened to his full height and looked down at her.

"Especially when what I have to say will offer another complication."

"What?"

MARRIAGE MASQUERADE | 93

"I think until the INS finishes its investigation, you need to share my room."

Stunned, Gemma widened her eyes. Had she heard him correctly?

"Share your room—your *bedroom?*"

"Phil went over some questions he suspects the investigator will ask. Like, have we consummated this marriage? Do we share a room? A bed? How long have we been in love? Did we date?"

Gemma couldn't have said a word if her life depended on it. She was looking forward to the sanctity of her bedroom at night. A place where she could escape Nikos' powerful attraction and magnetism for a while each day.

Now he wanted to take that away? Have her share his room?

He smiled, though no amusement showed in his eyes.

"Thanks. Your faith is overwhelming."

"I didn't say anything."

"Never play poker. Your expression gives away everything."

"That's not true. I have a great poker face. Look at how I do at work."

"Trust me, I could sense that you aren't thrilled with this complication."

She took a deep breath. The day was taking on a surreal atmosphere.

"What else? Might as well get everything out in the open.

Any other complications?"

"Would that be such a hardship? To sleep in my bed? It's quite large, and I don't move around a lot."

Sleep. A euphemism for making love.

Not that Nikos meant that. They'd merely sleep in the same bed. That huge king-size bed she'd glimpsed when touring the apartment.

"Okay. What else?"

"When around others, we need to act like we are a devoted couple."

"You said that before. What do you mean by devoted?"

He encircled her neck with one hand and pulled her closer.

"Touching, smiling into each other's eyes like we hold the secret of the universe."

He demonstrated, and Gemma's knees went weak.

What would she give to have a man look at her like this and mean it? She'd always wanted to fall in love and get married. Instead, she'd fallen in love with the wrong man and married a different one.

One who could capitalize on her vulnerability right now and lead her to imagine she was falling in love with him.

"You're not doing your part. Is this another instance where I have to ask?" he asked softly.

Slowly, Gemma relaxed. Gazing up into Nikos' eyes, she let a hint of emotion creep into hers. Smiling as seductively as she could, she reached up and brushed his lips with her fingertips.

"I'll give it my best shot, darling," she said huskily.

He groaned and stepped back.

"It's easier to deal with women in Greece than contrary Americans," he said, turning. He walked to the table and reached for his glass, draining the juice.

Feeling she'd held her own, Gemma didn't know how long she could hold out against the powerful pull of attraction her new husband engendered.

The sooner they got things back to normal, the better.

As if Nikos heard her thoughts and agreed with them, he became the perfect host to a guest in his home. The afternoon passed pleasantly as they explored superficial topics of conversation.

Hal prepared a wonderful meal for a wedding dinner, complete with champagne. Gemma took only a sip of hers.

"This is delicious," she murmured, wishing she dare drink more.

"My favorite aunt is from France. Her knowledge about fine wines is amazing. She's Allessandros's mother. You've met my cousin."

"Yes,."

"He has an American wife. I'll have to ask him for pointers."

She gave a mock frown. "A little consideration is all I'm asking."

He laughed and raised his flute.

"May all our days be as delightful as this one has been, Gemma."

Pleased with the toast, she touched her own glass to his and sipped.

Gemma hadn't expected a honeymoon. But Nikos had told her yesterday that he had planned for them both to take the rest of the week off from work. She was astonished when she rose the next morning to discover Nikos had left.

Weren't they both going to take the time off?

When she dressed and went to the dining room, Hal came in from the kitchen.

"I am to give you this note," he said when she asked where Nikos was.

Gemma opened the note and scanned the contents. Nikos had gone in for an errand. If she awoke before he returned, he hoped she'd make herself at home. Hal was available to prepare her breakfast.

And perhaps she'd move her things into his room. Tonight they'd share a bed to answer the INS's questions with all the honesty possible.

Another paragraph suggested she shop today for something to wear to the party. What was suitable for a personal assistant might not be suitable for his wife.

Gemma crumpled the note into a ball. If he'd been near, she'd blister his ears with her thoughts about his suggestions.

"Madam?"

"I'll take a poached egg on dry toast and some herbal tea."

"There is an assortment of teas already at the table. I'll bring you boiling water and prepare your breakfast."

Fuming, Gemma followed Hal into the dining room. How dare Nikos suggest her clothes were not suitable. They were stylish and of good quality.

Suitable for the wife of a wealthy international businessman? a voice inside whispered.

She sat and picked a packet of tea. Fixing the hot brew, she considered her options. She could feed her anger and let loose when he returned. Or she could go buy the most expensive dress she could find and charge it to him.

She didn't care that her reaction was childish. He made her so mad sometimes. It'd serve him right if she sent him the bill.

He won't mind, that voice said.

Which was probably true. He had enough money to buy any boutique she'd try with pocket change.

After dawdling over breakfast as long as she could, Gemma gave up waiting for Nikos. If he didn't care enough to return this morning, she'd put the time to good use.

Her first stop was the boutique she'd visited before. Recklessly, she told the saleswoman that she wanted the most outrageous dress they had. It would put a huge dint in her savings, but she didn't care.

Trying on dress after dress, none of them seemed exactly right. She wasn't sure what she was looking for—something to make a statement and drive the point home to her new husband.

When the salesclerk brought in a flame red dress, Gemma knew it was the one.

Trying it on, she crossed her fingers it would fit. She wasn't showing much in her pregnancy yet.

The dress slid over her like a second skin. It was one-shouldered, so that her left arm and shoulder were bare. It scarcely reached the top of her knees. Shimmering in the light, it was a sexy siren of a dress.

"Wow," she said.

"Wow is right," the saleswoman agreed. "If that doesn't get him to sit up and take notice, forget the man. He's dead."

Gemma glanced at her.

"You think this is for a man?"

"Why else?" the woman asked, amusement dancing in her eyes. "You want to tell me different?"

Gemma laughed. "No. I'll take it. Shoes?"

"We have some strappy high-heeled sandals in the exact shade that would be perfect for that dress. Let me see if we have your size."

While she waited, Gemma turned this way and that before

the mirror. She looked totally different, wild and free. And as unlike a staid personal assistant as it was possible to get.

Her heart sped up when she thought of Nikos' reaction when he saw her.

Throwing caution to the wind was fun, she decided. As long as she could handle things. Their understanding was firm. No falling in love on either side.

Katrina had burned him, just as James had burned her.

They had a mutually beneficial agreement that suited them both.

"Try these." The saleswoman handed Gemma the shoes.

They were perfect.

Gemma hummed happily as she changed back into her street clothes.

As the salesclerk wrapped the dress and shoes, she glanced at Gemma hesitantly.

"I'm stepping out of line with this, but I would suggest a new hairstyle. Something short and sassy that will complement the dress. Or have it done up in an elaborate cascade?"

Gemma nodded. It was worth thinking about.

Hadn't Nikos just yesterday said he liked her hair around her face?

Not that she would change her hairstyle because of his comment. But another style would go better with the dress.

Gemma hurried back to the apartment, placing her new dress in her closet. She spent part of the afternoon moving her other clothes to Nikos' closet. And to the drawers Hal had cleared for her.

Feeling odd about sharing the space, Gemma left as soon as everything was put away.

Where was Nikos?

She phoned the office and learned that he had gone in for a short meeting and was involved.

It was late by the time Gemma heard the door to the apartment open. She had given in to Hal's entreaties and eaten hours earlier.

Nikos appeared in the doorway to the living room. Gemma put down her book.

"Tough day?" she asked.

He looked tired. She had never noticed that before. Was she growing more attuned to the man?

"More so than usual."

He loosened his tie and shrugged out of his suit jacket.

"Go change, and I'll get Hal to fix your dinner. I already ate."

"I hoped you would."

He hesitated a minute, then nodded. "I won't be long. I didn't mean to desert you on our first day together. But the negotiations need to get out of the logjam or we'll be stalemated when the contract expires."

"I know that."

He nodded.

"I missed my personal assistant today."

"Nice to be appreciated. Maybe I should hit you up for a raise next Monday."

"Maybe I'll give you one without being asked."

Gemma smiled as she listened to him walk down the hallway. One more weekday to play honeymooner, then they'd be back at work on Monday and things would be as close to normal as they'd get for the next few months.

Nikos brought her up-to-date on the situation while eating dinner. She realized she'd worried he would close her out of the loop once they married. But he didn't.

"Tomorrow morning, we have the interview with the Immigration Department. And the party in the evening," Nikos said.

"I have an appointment to have my hair done in the afternoon," she mentioned casually.

Would he like her hair short? Or did he like it long? Doubts assailed her.

They were chased away when it came time to retire. Tonight Gemma was sleeping in Nikos' bed. With him. Tomorrow could take care of itself. She had tonight to worry about.

When he said he wanted to check his messages in his home office, Gemma took the time to hurry to the bedroom. Clad in a full-length nightgown that tied at the neck and had long lacy sleeves, she slid into the bed and clung to the edge.

She wasn't sure which side she should sleep on, but took a hint from the clock by the far side. Surely it was placed so he could silence the alarm each morning.

Despite the worry about the sleeping arrangement and tomorrow's pending meeting, Gemma fell asleep long before Nikos joined her.

The next morning the bed showed signs of his occupancy, but Nikos was already up when she awoke.

Stretching, she reached out to touch the pillow he'd used. He had been right, darn him. Nothing had happened, and the bed was plenty large enough for them both. She'd never known he'd joined her last night.

Dressing, she hurried to the dining room. Nikos had finished eating and was sipping coffee as he read the paper.

"Good morning. I hope I'm not late," Gemma said as she took the chair to his right.

"We have plenty of time. Phil told me yesterday they'd probably interrogate us separately."

"Oh. Okay, I guess. What are we saying?"

"We've worked together for five years. During that time, we've grown close. Not realizing how close until it looked as if I was being deported. Then you confessed your love for me and I said—"

"Wait a minute. I confessed my love for you? Try it the other way around."

"Now's not a time to be contrary."

"It works just as well the other way. You found out you were being deported and hated to go—not because of work, that would get done with your excellent managers—but because you'd have to leave me."

She smiled brightly. "I really think that is much better."

Nikos frowned, but gave the matter serious consideration. "Maybe you're right. It takes the emphasis off the business."

"I'll want a really large raise," she said smugly.

Three hours later, Nikos and Gemma entered a cab in front of the Immigration Building. He settled back as the driver slid into the busy traffic.

She leaned closer to whisper in his ear.

"I think we pulled it off, don't you? It went so smoothly."

He nodded, his eyes on the cabdriver. The man ignored them as he fought the heavy midtown traffic.

Nikos looked at Gemma. She was glowing with happiness. There was more to go through, but she was right—it looked as if the inspector believed their story. Of course, bringing in her pregnancy helped. Nikos knew the man thought the child was his.

For a moment, he wondered what it'd be like to be a father. To take turns rocking a cranky baby, or to watch his wife nurse their child at her breast. To watch Gemma shower her love on the baby.

Her scent reached him, light and fragrant. Lilacs, he

thought. He was used to it, for she wore it all the time. Used to it, but attracted just the same.

Blast it, he found that happening more and more. When had Gemma changed from a perfect personal assistant to a woman who captured his attention?

She'd been giving and passionate in the kisses they'd shared. Yet last night, despite the warmth in the apartment, she had worn a virginal gown to bed that covered her from head to foot. At least, he imagined it was long.

She'd had a warm flush on her face when he finally joined her in the bedroom. He'd watched her sleep for several long moments, trying to figure out what had changed between them.

And why he was feeling a need to know more about her, to touch her, to feel the delicate texture of her skin.

Why he wanted to kiss her. Why he wanted her.

He looked out the cab's window. Things had changed, but he hadn't. Hadn't Katrina proved women wanted what men could give them, but not the men themselves?

In this situation, Gemma was no different. She wanted an escape from embarrassment because of her unexpected pregnancy.

He'd better never forget that. No matter how much he might want her.

"I've changed my mind, driver," Nikos said, giving him the office address.

To Gemma he said, "Since you'll be busy this afternoon, I might as well go in to the office for a few hours."

To escape the temptation that was growing when he was around her. The temptation to kiss her, to learn more about her. To make her his wife in every way.

Chapter Six

Gemma hesitated, staring at her reflection in the mirror. She almost didn't recognize herself. She'd slipped into the apartment earlier, seeing no one. Using the guest bathroom, she prepared for the party. Now she was ready. Or as ready as she was going to get. Could she pull this off?

It wasn't really her. Just part of this weird dance she was doing with Nikos. Her hair was a froth of curls, framing her face, softening it. Making her eyes look huge.

Or was it the new makeup the stylist had suggested? Gemma wasn't sure, but she looked different. Mysterious, interesting, almost sexy.

The red lipstick matched her dress. As did her fingernails and toenails. The dress hadn't looked so blatantly sexy in the boutique, had it? Had she put on weight? Or had it been this skintight yesterday?

Swallowing hard and taking a deep breath, she wondered for the millionth time what Nikos would say.

"No time like the present to find out," she said, taking another deep breath.

Many more and she'd hyperventilate. Throwing open the door, she raised her head, threw back her shoulders and walked boldly out.

Down the hall, into the living room—her heart beating a rapid tempo.

Nikos stood near the windows. He did that a lot, she noticed. Did he feel confined in buildings?

She must have made some noise, because he turned. And stared.

Almost smiling, Gemma felt giddy with unexpected delight. After five years of working together, she'd finally surprised him.

"Gemma?"

Sashaying into the room with a bravado she didn't feel, she nodded.

"You said you liked my hair around my face, so I got it cut to do just that."

Darn, she hadn't meant to let that slip. That was not the reason she got her hair cut. She liked the short style and the loose curls that now framed her face. It was a sassy look, one she would never have tried before. But somehow it seemed right for tonight's event.

"Did I also say I liked you in red? What there almost is of that dress," he said, his gaze roving over every inch of her. Did he linger on certain areas?

The familiar flutter began. She needn't worry about being

cold in the dress. The heat that swept through her at his look would keep her warm in a snowstorm.

"Not red particularly, but you said you were tired of black. Are you ready to go?"

He hesitated for a long moment. Then nodded curtly.

"Hal has the car down in front. Do you have a coat or something to wear with that?"

"Yes, it's by the door."

Impulsively she stepped closer and reached up to pat his collar, brush an imaginary speck of lint from his shoulder. What was she trying to prove?

The edge of his hand lifted her chin. Nikos lowered his head until his face was only inches from hers, his breath caressing her cheeks. The dark glitter in his eyes had her pulse racing.

"What are you doing?" he asked in a low, husky voice.

A dozen answers trembled on her lips. She went with honesty.

"I'm trying to act the part of a devoted wife of a worldly man," she said.

Her lips seemed to tingle. Would he close those scant few inches and kiss her?

"Ah, I wondered."

He straightened and offered his arm. "Shall we?"

Disappointed, she hid it, smiling brightly.

The reception was in full swing by the time they arrived.

A uniformed maid took Gemma's coat. It was one thing to wear the dress in the safety of their apartment, but quite something else to walk into a room of strangers.

For a long moment she hesitated at the entrance to the wide ballroom.

Gemma had never been the belle of any ball, but for an instant, she knew what it felt like. Men stopped and stared, smiles of appreciation lighting their features. Women discreetly assessed her dress and hairstyle. From some frowns, Gemma wasn't sure if they disapproved or were envious.

Raising her chin, she hoped she was equal to the task she'd set. She'd hate herself in the morning if she made a fool of herself at Nikos' expense.

Nikos introduced her to their host, got a glass of ginger ale for her, and gently steered her toward a group of men he wanted to speak with. Though his touch was light at the small of her back, Gemma's skin heated. She tried to ignore the sensation and concentrated on making a good impression on his colleagues.

Greeting the men, some of whom she knew, she fell silent, content to listen to the conversation swirling around her without having to take part. It was an interesting topic, the latest international business trends. She'd pick up key points, which would assist in her job.

When Nikos spoke, she noticed how often the others deferred to his opinions and seemed to value his input. She, too, valued his opinions, though she was more likely to argue with them when the occasion arose. He didn't want to surround himself with yes-men, and Gemma made it clear that she'd never be counted as one.

"What about you, Gemma? What is a woman's take on all this?" one man asked.

Thinking carefully before she spoke, Gemma was gratified to find the same attention was paid to what she said. Though one or two of the men obviously disagreed, no one contradicted her.

"And who is this fascinating creature who has the men hanging on her every word?"

A tall, statuesque blonde joined the group, her eyes surveying each man as if he was her special property. Smiling at Nikos, she extended her hand.

"I don't believe we've met. I'm Sally Rogers."

Nikos shook her hand briefly. "Nikos Petropoulos. My wife, Gemma."

For a moment, the blonde's confidence wavered, but she recovered quickly.

"How nice."

"It is for me," Gemma said, stepping closer to Nikos.

She knew she couldn't compete with the women he used to date, but for now, he was off-limits to all other women. And Gemma meant to reinforce that.

What was she doing, thinking of Nikos as hers? Theirs

was a business arrangement, a marriage to suit them both. Not some grand love affair that excluded the rest of the world.

Gemma wondered what it'd be like to be caught up in blazing passion and devoted love for real instead of a masquerade they were displaying to the world.

When Nikos' hand rested on her bare shoulder, she almost jumped. Then she smiled and turned to him, hoping the confusion of her thoughts didn't show in her eyes.

"Would you care for something to eat?" he asked softly, turning slightly from the group.

"Yes, I'm starving."

"I've noticed how you enjoy your meals," he said as he excused them and headed for the lavish buffet on tables at the far wall.

"I need to keep up my strength."

"Ah, eating for two, I believe the saying goes."

"Actually, I was thinking more of keeping up with you. Do you think I came across too strongly in that group? I noticed a couple of men seemed annoyed."

"You expressed yourself well. Morganstern didn't like your opinion, but you wouldn't let that stop you from voicing it, would you?"

"No."

Nikos spoke to several people in passing, and Gemma wondered if he knew everyone present.

When another woman stopped him, Gemma felt her heart

sink. She'd thought Sally Rogers beautiful, but this woman made Sally look like a gauche high-school girl.

"Stunning" was the only term to describe her.

Depressed, Gemma watched while Nikos' former wife greeted him.

"Hello, darling," the woman said, reaching up to kiss Nikos with a familiarity that had Gemma frowning.

Nikos stepped back, his expression impassive.

"Katrina. I didn't know you would be here."

"Obviously, darling. Justin thought it would be a pleasant diversion for us to attend. Have you seen the paintings Sven bought from his protégé? Intriguing work. I believe he'll be a tremendous success."

Katrina let her gaze move to Gemma. There was a tightness around the eyes, but beyond that, her smile seemed almost genuine.

"Gemma, are you Nikos' date for the evening?"

"No, Katrina, Gemma's my wife."

Her shocked look proved she hadn't heard about Nikos' marriage.

Gemma felt a hint of smug satisfaction at the woman's startled expression.

Katrina's gaze swung back to his. "You married again?"

"I was free to do so."

"To her?" she asked, as if Gemma was totally beyond the realm of possibility.

Nikos smiled at Gemma, winking with his left eye.

"Yes, to Gemma. Wish us well, Katrina. We're having a baby."

Shocked, Katrina looked back and forth, as if trying to fathom the words she'd heard.

"And my wife's hungry. If you'll excuse us."

He took Gemma's arm gently and urged her on their way toward the buffet table.

Gemma felt the tension shimmering in the air.

"She's still lovely," she murmured, feeling she ought to say something.

The spurt of jealousy that gripped her hadn't abated. But there was nothing for her to be concerned about. It wasn't as if Nikos had any interest in Katrina.

"I didn't know she would be here. Sven knows I don't like to even be in the same room with her."

"Who is Justin?"

"I don't know. Her latest, I guess. I don't really care."

Nikos' anger simmered just below the surface. Nikos' fury was clear to Gemma, even though he had a firm hold on his emotions.

"What would you like to eat?"

They had reached the buffet tables, and from the tone of his voice, Gemma knew further conversation about his beautiful ex-wife was closed.

When they finished nibbling at some hors d'oeuvres,

Nikos introduced Gemma to another couple and they chatted for a few minutes. Then one of the men Gemma had met earlier joined them.

"Can I borrow Gemma for a moment? Morganstern has finally come up with what he thinks are sound reasons to repute her views on that global trend. I want to see if Gemma can defend herself."

At Nikos' nod, she put down her glass and crossed the room. In only moments, she was embroiled in a debate with the older man who didn't agree with her. Stretching her mental abilities, she countered all his arguments, stating hers calmly and with conviction.

Soon the others in the group were laughing and rooting for her. The debate cooled, and the topic changed.

Nikos joined her.

"Pretty wife you've got there, Nikos," one man said genially.

"Smart, too," Morganstern growled, not looking at all displeased.

"I agree. If you gentlemen will excuse us?"

He took Gemma's hand, threading his fingers through hers.

When they were out of hearing, he glanced at her, anger once again simmering.

"I do not expect to find my wife flirting with other men at parties. It was unacceptable with Katrina, and it is unacceptable with you."

Shocked, Gemma stopped and turned to face him. Her own indignation was immediate.

"Just a minute. I wasn't flirting with anyone."

"And what was all that laughing at Morganstern's stupid jokes and exchanging amused glances with Peterson?"

"Which one was Peterson?"

"You don't even know the man's name, but you can flirt with him?"

"I hardly call being cordial at a party flirting."

"And I hardly call it circumspect. What if the INS has an agent here? What would he think of our marriage?"

Narrowing her eyes, Gemma studied Nikos.

"Let me guess. Knowing what little I do about Katrina, I imagine she's the type to demand constant attention from the opposite sex. Are you suggesting that I'm at all like that? After having worked together, I would expect a bit more faith from you."

"And what would you call your behavior?"

"Making a good impression so men will be envious of you for having married me," she said swiftly.

Slowly the tension faded from Nikos' expression. He began to smile.

Gemma's knees grew wobbly, her heart thudded in her chest, and she felt like she might melt into a puddle at Nikos' feet. How could just a smile turn her bones to jelly and her mind to mush?

"And do all those men now envy me?"

She shrugged, looking away before she did something foolish, like flinging herself into his arms and demanding he take them home so she could escape the stress of the party and the constant need to guard against making a major mistake.

"I only know what they think about the international banking situation and the recession in Japan. But I hope they think I'm more than some bit of fluff you picked up," she said with some asperity.

"Are we talking about Katrina again?"

Hearing a hint of amusement in his voice, she dared another look in his direction. His dark eyes danced.

"If the shoe fits."

"I apologize if I misread the situation. Let's mingle so more people here can meet you and be envious of my good fortune."

Gemma knew Nikos was teasing her, but she didn't mind. Despite her trepidation about the evening, she was having a wonderful time.

Nikos remained attentive throughout the rest of their evening, displaying all the pride of a newly married man. She tried not to wish it was true, instead of make-believe.

If she let herself forget for a single minute the reason for their union, Gemma knew she could become swept away by the enigmatic man. His charm was deep and dangerous. Playing a part was only one step from living a part.

And she was finding it more and more difficult to remember it was only a charade.

By the time they left, Gemma was exhausted. If this was what she could expect when they went out, she'd do her best to see they stayed home as much as possible.

"Did you enjoy yourself?" Nikos asked, one finger idly toying with a curl of her hair.

They were sitting in the back of the limousine while Hal drove swiftly through the dark streets.

"More than I thought I would. But I'm not much for big gatherings like that."

She began to relax. The evening was behind her, and she hadn't made a single faux pas.

But how could anyone relax with Nikos so close? With his fingers in her hair? His scent surrounding her?

"You handled yourself well. We'll be obligated to attend a certain number of similar functions during the year. In the future, I'll consult you before having Elise send an acceptance."

Gemma smiled, despite the flutters his touch brought. "Thank you."

"I think our being married is going to be an interesting time for however long our journey lasts."

"Journey?"

"To our final destination."

"Which is?"

"That's part of the interesting aspect—we don't know the final destination yet."

Gemma knew where an interim destination would be if Nikos didn't stop touching her, toying with her hair.

But she wasn't ready for something like that. Until a few weeks ago, she'd thought herself in love with James. No, she *had* been in love with him. His deceit had killed it instantly. But it would be safer to go through life without the complications of falling for another man. Especially one who'd never love her in return.

Even one as exciting as Nikos.

Hal delivered them to the door and drove off to park the car. Gemma followed Nikos into the elevator, her nerves stretched tighter every second as the car silently rose to their floor.

Nikos let them into their apartment. Hal had propped up a note on the small entryway table. Nikos picked it up as Gemma shed her coat.

"Important?" she asked.

"Probably not, or Hal would have mentioned it in the car. It's a message from my father," Nikos said.

He skimmed the words again and shrugged.

"It seems Allessandros discovered our marriage and informed my father. He wishes to speak with me."

Gemma almost giggled. She caught her lower lip between her teeth. Nikos made it sound like he was a recalcitrant teenager about to be hauled on the carpet.

"I take it you didn't tell your parents," she said when the danger of the giggles had passed.

"Not as yet." He glanced at his watch. "It's morning there. I'll phone him now."

"Then I guess I'll head for bed."

Nikos watched her hurry down the hall almost regretfully. He didn't want the night to end. He knew she'd be in bed before he finished his phone call. Either asleep or feigning sleep.

Should he call her on it tonight? Talk to her in the dark, learn more about the woman than what he thought he knew from working with her?

After the way she attacked Morganstern's antiquated ideas, she could obviously hold her own in various situations. Yet she still acted like a skittish filly around him.

Pretending to be a devoted couple was wearing on a man, especially when his wife kept that bright smile trained in his direction. What would Gemma do if he kissed her, ran his hands over that sexy body, felt the heat of her skin, the softness of its texture?

Her hair felt like silk. How would her skin all over feel?

A man could only withstand so much temptation before giving in. And he'd been a long time without a woman. He wondered if he'd ever made love to such a contradiction of shyness and boldness. Her dress caused quite a stir tonight, yet the shy innocence that shone from her eyes was a direct challenge. One he wanted to take on.

First, however, he needed to talk to his father. He knew the man would be disappointed he hadn't told him about his marriage.

How Allessandros had discovered it was another question.

As Nikos had suspected, his father was upset. He tried to explain the situation, but his father insisted there would have been other ways to comply with the American rules and regulations regarding the visa situation.

He questioned his son's motive for marrying yet another foreigner.

"Did you not learn your lesson with Katrina?" Stephanos Petropoulos roared.

"Gemma's different," Nikos defended, keeping his voice low and calm.

His father had a tendency to exaggerate everything, and Nikos knew from years of experience that someone had to keep a cool head.

"I shall be the judge of that. Bring her here so I can meet her."

"Not yet, Father. If I could take a trip home without jeopardizing the negotiations, I would have returned to get a visa."

"How are the negotiations proceeding?"

Diverted, he questioned his son on the progress with the union. Only after the negotiations were settled in their favor did he once again insist on his son going home.

Nikos hung up the phone and leaned back in his desk chair. Dealing with his father never got easier. The man was absolute ruler in his household, and getting him to change his mind about anything required a certain finesse Nikos wondered if he'd ever master.

He should take lessons from his mother. She seemed to get whatever she wanted from her husband. Not that she ever asked for much.

Maybe that was the key.

Everything she asked for was important to her, and her husband was pleased to indulge her to bring her happiness.

What would bring Gemma happiness? Nikos wondered.

Separate bedrooms, he suspected, frowning.

A quick end to their mock marriage?

Three days of wedded bliss was not enough time to see how they'd deal together in the future. He thought he knew her from the years she'd worked for him. Tonight, though, she'd totally surprised him. Would there be other surprises?

Delightful ones or distressful ones?

The adventure of marriage was not something he'd considered after divorcing Katrina. He didn't like the games and the constant need to be on guard.

Yet with Gemma, he felt it would be different. Vastly different. And that held a certain appeal.

Anticipating seeing her in the morning, he rose and headed for their room. He knew she'd be asleep, but just in case she wasn't...

Gemma looked up from the toast she was buttering when Nikos joined her in the dining room the next morning.

"Good morning," she said, carefully resuming her task. She'd been disappointed when she awoke to find Nikos had already risen. Not that she expected him to stay in bed until she woke.

"Did you sleep well?" he inquired.

"Yes."

Nikos sat at the head of the table and poured himself some coffee. As if he'd been listening behind the door, Hal entered with a plate of steaming eggs and sausage.

Gemma helped herself and began to eat.

"Allessandros and his wife have invited us to visit next weekend," Nikos said when Hal left.

"In Washington?"

"Yes. We can fly down next Saturday morning and return on Sunday evening."

"That's a quick visit."

"You would prefer longer?"

"No, that's fine. I met Allessandros. I look forward to meeting his wife."

"They're both eager to get to know you."

Gemma looked up at the tone in his voice. "In what way?"

"Just vetting a new wife," Nikos said.

"Maybe I don't want to be vetted. You told them this is temporary, right?" she asked.

He looked at her.

"Slipped my mind."

"Your mind's like a steel trap. Why didn't you tell them?"

"They don't need to know."

"What happens when we separate?"

Nikos shrugged.

"Time enough to deal with that when it comes. Hal had the furniture you wanted moved here yesterday. The pieces are in the spare bedroom at the end of the hall. Have you seen them?" he asked, changing the subject.

"He told me this morning the pieces are all in one room."

"So today we'll place them where you wish."

Mocking him gently, she inclined her head the way he did. "As you wish."

The glint in his eye told her he noticed and chose not to comment.

The day turned out to be fun for Gemma.

Neither Nikos nor Hal would allow her to lift anything. Once Hal got over his astonishment that Nikos planned to take part in the actual moving of the furniture, he grew more at ease in their presence, though never crossing the bounds of propriety.

Gemma carefully studied each room and had each piece placed where she thought it would enhance the existing arrangement. With various pieces of her furniture throughout the apartment, she felt more at home.

Two odd chairs remained. Studying them with a critical eye, she knew they'd have to go.

"Sorry you moved these, Hal. They are too tacky to stay."

"Tacky?"

"Ugly, unsuitable." She sighed and sat on one. "And uncomfortable. I don't know why I had them moved."

Hal glided away as the doorbell rang. Gemma looked at Nikos.

"Are you expecting company? I look a mess."

"I'm not expecting anyone."

He moved to the archway and listened.

"Ah, the immigration inspector, if I'm not mistaken."

He held out his hand and drew Gemma to her feet.

"Let's go and get inspected."

The agent from INS stayed only an hour, looked into every aspect of the apartment and asked numerous questions—some of which had been asked at their offices the previous morning.

When he left, he mentioned he thought everything was in order. There were a few more technicalities, but it looked in all likelihood that they'd recommend the resident visa.

Gemma waited until the door closed behind him and then clapped her hands.

"We did it."

"Perhaps. Did you notice he never quite said it was a done deal? When I have the green card in hand, then we'll know we did it."

"I think it's a done deal. And you know what tipped the scales, don't you?" she asked when Nikos merely shrugged.

"What?"

"My looking terrible today. You'd have to love me to put up with this."

He ran a fingertip along her cheek, tracing her jaw.

"I would, would I?"

Closing the distance, he kissed her.

The unexpected embrace caught her unaware. Gemma leaned back against the wall to keep from falling. After her initial surprise, she savored the feel of Nikos' lips against hers, relished the sensations that cascaded through her. She opened her lips to respond and was swept away in a vortex of sensations and swirling excitement.

When he straightened, she gazed up into his dark eyes, glad for the support of the wall, wondering if he could hear the thundering of her heart. What was he thinking? Did the kisses mean anything? Or was it just for the moment? Was she just convenient?

"Even though he reported it looks likely he'd recommend the permanent visa, I say we continue our vigilance until it's in hand," Nikos said slowly, lightly tracing her jaw with a finger.

He met her gaze and cocked an eyebrow.

"I believe we need to keep up the devoted-couple bit—to fool the INS, of course."

"I think they're fooled," she said. "And I doubt they'll be back here again."

"Ah, you wish to make some change?"

Restlessly, she pushed away and paced the room. "I don't think we need to continue sharing a bed. I can leave my clothes in the closet for a while, but we've been questioned twice. Do you really think they will do it again?"

Not meeting his eyes, she rubbed her arms and continued to pace.

She wasn't sure she could resist the powerful pull of attraction being around Nikos provoked. She'd slipped off to bed before him for a couple of nights, but how long could she keep it up? How long before she rolled over in the night and snuggled against his muscular body? How long could she resist temptation before throwing caution to the wind and asking him to kiss her? To make love to his wife?

And what would happen if she was still wide awake when he joined her in that bed? Even though it was large, it was not that large. Look at how big the room was, yet she was acutely aware of Nikos' every move.

Risking a quick look, she found his expression bland. What did he think of her demand?

"Your choice," he said.

Abruptly, he turned and left the room.

"Well, you got what you wanted," she murmured,

wondering why she felt so disappointed.

Chapter Seven

Gemma gazed out the airplane window as the tall spire of the Washington Monument came into view. She glanced at Nikos. He was still engrossed in the report he'd brought along to study. Turning back to the small window, she wondered what this visit would bring.

Would Allessandros grill her on why she'd married his cousin? Find her lacking in the attributes the family would wish for Nikos' wife? She knew it was a temporary arrangement, but Nikos' family did not.

Or had Nikos told Allessandros the reason for their hasty wedding? Would they be disappointed in his choice of a wife?

She hoped not. She wanted his family to like her.

This past week had been odd. During the day, she felt no different from how she'd felt for the past five years. Except for a strong sense of awareness of Nikos that hadn't been present before.

She hoped she had hidden that from him, but with his uncanny ability to cut to the key aspect in business dealings, she worried she'd given herself away.

The evenings had been a different story. Those they spent together. Awkwardly at first, like strangers trying to grope their way through the stages of learning about one another. As the week progressed, Gemma knew she'd learned more about her enigmatic husband than she'd gleaned over all the years they'd worked together.

And what little she had learned confused her.

Nikos was a curious blend of his Greek heritage and American ways. While he paid lip service to women's rights, Gemma suspected if he could have things entirely his way, his word would be law.

She challenged him over inconsequential things just for the impish joy of watching him as he drew on his strength of resolve and marshaled his arguments.

By Thursday, he'd caught her out.

Gemma smiled dreamily as she gazed at the approaching airport.

He'd been furious. Or had that been just for her benefit? She still thought she'd seen a twinkle of amusement in his dark eyes for all his arguments.

The kisses he'd showered on her hadn't been amusing. Exciting, tumultuous, wildly exotic, but definitely not amusing. She grew warm remembering.

If Hal had not interrupted, would those kisses have led to something more?

Sometimes she regretted making an issue of moving into

her own room after Immigration's home inspection. Not that she expected anything from her husband. He'd not touched her the two nights she'd shared that enormous bed. Would her remaining there have changed anything?

Did she really want to change things? It wasn't as if their marriage was real or they planned to continue it. A physical intimacy would complicate matters, she knew. But that knowledge didn't stop her yearning. Just for a kind word, a gentle caress. A passionate kiss.

Be grateful for what you have, *she scolded herself.*

But sometimes she wished she hadn't told him about James. Even fantasized once or twice that they had married because of mutual desire.

Though their marriage was unconventional, she liked it.

What would it be like if Nikos had wooed her and won her? Courted her with flowers, dinners out, dancing? Pledged himself to her for all time?

She shook her head and sighed. He'd made his position clear enough. He didn't trust women. And she was realistic enough to know that if his visa hadn't lapsed, he'd never have thought of marrying her—or anyone else.

After seeing Katrina's reaction at the party, she wondered how much the woman regretted losing Nikos. Had she wanted to rekindle his affections?

Or had theirs been a mercenary arrangement from the beginning?

How could she not be attracted to the man? And regret the ending of their relationship?

Gemma couldn't imagine being more interested in Nikos' fortune than the man himself.

"Well, she can't have him," Gemma murmured, startled by the strength of her feelings.

"What?"

Nikos looked at her.

"Nothing. I was just thinking aloud. We're almost there."

She kept her gaze firmly out the window, lest he suspect what she'd said. She needed to watch her tongue.

He slid the papers back into the file and placed it into his briefcase. When he placed it beneath the seat in front of him, Gemma turned to watch.

"Did the Alteras report have what you were looking for?" she asked.

The small firm was a subsidiary of ALK Shipping and recently acquired.

"The returns are higher than expected."

"Which means Johnson's doing a good job there. I know you had doubts when you gave him the manager's position."

"It's early yet. But yes, I think he's showing more potential than I originally expected." Nikos raised an eyebrow. "Are you going to say you told me so?"

Gemma grinned. "Why, I didn't know you thought I was the type to gloat when proved right."

"Proved right? You voiced approval of Johnson's appointment, but the proof is far from in."

"The way you go, it'll be fifty years before you let yourself admit he's a good choice."

"I believe in accepting responsibility for my decisions, however they turn out."

"I hope you regret none of them," she said, glancing at her wedding band.

"If you are referring to our marriage, I accept responsibility for that as well. Time will tell if it proves successful."

"Do we wait fifty years to find out?"

Gemma almost slapped her hand over her mouth after the words came out. She stared at him wide-eyed. It sounded too much like she wanted to stay married. It was one thing to fantasize about being courted, and quite another to verbalize it.

Nikos' expression changed almost imperceptibly, became more guarded.

"We could wait fifty years. Are you considering staying with me that long?"

For a moment she was speechless as the realization flooded. She wanted to stay with him. She liked and respected him. If she was totally honest, she'd enjoyed the week and a half since they'd been married. She knew she could depend on him to do the right thing, no matter what the cost to himself. He'd see that he was a good, reliable husband. Someone she could count on.

But how did he feel?

For a wild, giddy moment, Gemma considered the possibility of staying married. Could they make it work? The romantic personal assistant from Ohio and the businessman billionaire from Greece?

Slowly, reality intruded.

Even if they continued, she didn't want a lopsided relationship, with her growing fonder and fonder of Nikos while he continued his own way.

"We'll see," she temporized, afraid of the sudden suspicion that plagued her.

She was growing too fond of her boss. Too intrigued with the idea of staying with him for the rest of her life. Too involved with watching him when he didn't know she was looking, listening to him as if she'd never heard him before. And she was growing too dependent. Time to distance herself. Hadn't she learned her lesson?

Yet Nikos was unlike any other man she'd ever known. There was an innate honesty and honor about the man. Almost old-worldly. A blend of the cultures, maybe. But captivating and comforting. She knew beyond any doubt he'd live up to his word. He'd never lie or deceive someone—

especially someone he cared about.

She couldn't be falling in love with him. This was just a rebound thing or something.

She didn't want to fall in love again. It was too risky for her heart.

And with someone like Nikos, even more so.

Yet…

The plane bumped gently down.

"Oh, we're here already," Gemma said, glad of the interruption of her tumbling thoughts.

How would she fit in with Nikos' family? Would they all know instantly she was a fraud?

"Allessandros will meet us at baggage claim. You've heard me mention his wife, Megan. He has a daughter named Norrie, and a son called Sam."

"Sam?" Gemma frowned. That didn't sound very Greek to her.

"Actually, his full name is Aristotle Pierre Petropoulos. Remember Allessandros's mother is French? But for some reason unbeknownst to me, they have called him Sam since his birth."

Feeling shy about the prospect of spending a weekend with Nikos' family, Gemma followed Nikos up the jetway and into the airport.

Allessandros, tall and imposing, stood to one side of the crowded baggage claim area, waiting.

Unconsciously, Gemma compared the two men. Their self-confidence was amazing. And they were charming when it suited them.

The cousins greeted each other with back slaps and grins.

Allessandros turned to her and smiled. He inclined his head in a manner similar to Nikos.

"Welcome to our family, Gemma Petropoulos."

"Thank you."

Flustered, she looked to Nikos for support. She felt awful about their charade. How would Allessandros feel when the truth all came out?

To Gemma's surprise, there was no chauffeur. Allessandros drove.

The luxurious Mercedes was a delight. Gemma insisted on sitting in the back while the two men sat in the front and caught up on family business.

She ran her hand lovingly over the rich leather and sighed in contentment. She'd better not grow too used to such luxury, she thought, but it'd be nice while it lasted.

When Allessandros turned into a short driveway some time later, the house was not what she expected. Instead of an enormous mansion surrounded by acres of manicured lawns, the modest ranch style home sat in the center of an ordinary middle-class neighborhood. She expected something more palatial.

Even Nikos seemed surprised.

"You live here?"

Allessandros raised an eyebrow.

"You have a problem with my home?"

"No. Just…it's different from what I expected."

"This was Megan's home before we married. Her parents moved to the southwest, and we bought the home. It's becoming crowded now. But when we first married, I don't think she quite trusted our marriage would last and wanted something of her own as insurance. Now we're used to it. But when the baby comes, we'll definitely need something larger."

"Megan's expecting again?" Nikos asked as he climbed from the car and held the back door for Gemma.

At Allessandros' nod, he looked at Gemma.

"Something else you will have in common with Megan."

"The first thing being?" Gemma asked, flicking a glance at Nikos.

He'd told his cousin she was pregnant? Had he told him about the full circumstances?

"Being married to a sexy Greek man, of course."

"Of course," Gemma said dryly, smiling despite her wish to look insulted.

"Nikos. How nice to see you again."

A tall woman and a teenage girl, looking remarkably alike, smiled broadly as they moved to greet him.

Nikos straightened and, taking Gemma's hand in his, walked forward to greet Megan and Norrie.

"You've grown another six inches, I am sure, since I last saw you," Nikos said as he gave the girl a hug, then held her away from him to study her.

"Not true, but I'm losing some of that baby fat, so I look taller, don't I, Daddy?" she asked her father.

Allessandros exchanged an amused glance with his wife and nodded.

"And this must be Gemma. I'm Megan. I'm so glad you came. We'll have a great weekend. Come on in. Sam's asleep, but he'll be awake soon. How was your trip?"

"Fine."

Gemma was swept along with their enthusiasm. Her nervousness vanished in the light of Megan's friendliness. Maybe the weekend would be fun, after all.

She glanced over her shoulder. Nikos and Allessandros stood by the car, their voices low as they talked.

Following Megan, Gemma was pleased that Norrie kept pace with her.

"Nikos said you lived right in Manhattan before you got married. I would love to visit New York. I think the stores there would offer a ton of cool things," Norrie said excitedly. "We've been only once. Maybe you and Nikos would invite me up to visit."

Megan laughed and chided her daughter.

"They don't want company just yet. I already told you we would get up there at least once before the baby comes."

"That's weeks away," she said, wrinkling her nose. "Nikos said you were pregnant—did you know my mom's pregnant, too?" Norrie asked as they entered the house. "I'm hoping for a girl this time, but Mom says all she cares about is that it's a healthy child. And she won't find out ahead of time. Do you know what you're having yet?"

Gemma shook her head. With a start, she realized she had thought little about the baby beyond being pregnant. Of course, the past week had been taken up with Nikos. But in only a few months, she'd be a mother with a baby totally dependent upon her.

Would she still be married to Nikos? Or would they have ended their marriage by then? Once he received his green card, the need to remain married would end.

How long would that take, she wondered.

She didn't want to end it. Didn't want to be on her own, coping with work and a baby and the loneliness. Susan wouldn't want a baby to share their small apartment.

During the past week, Gemma had found she loved sitting in the evenings talking, listening to music and relaxing in a living room that was so different from what she was used to.

She'd miss that when their arrangement ended.

"Hush, Norrie, let Gemma get her breath. Do you wish to freshen up after your flight? I'll show you where you'll be staying tonight."

Megan led the way down a short hall.

"Allessandros agrees we need a larger place when the baby comes. This is only a three-bedroom house. Here, you and Nikos will have Norrie's room for the night."

Megan paused at the doorway of a light, airy room. An organdy spread that matched the curtains on the windows covered the bed.

It was a teenager's room with all the things a young girl cherished—from a purple stuffed animal on one shelf to posters of movie stars pinned to the walls.

But Gemma didn't notice the decorations—she focused on the bed.

The small double bed.

This was nothing like the king-size bed Nikos had in his bedroom. This one looked scarcely large enough for two people to squeeze in without falling to the floor.

Gemma felt a touch of panic. She'd barely made it through two nights with Nikos with acres of room between them. In this tiny bed she'd get no sleep, no rest.

She couldn't do it.

"Is something wrong?" Norrie asked.

Gemma dragged her gaze away from the bed and tried to smile at the teenager.

"Everything's fine. Your room is lovely. I just hate for you to give it up for us."

She had to talk to Nikos. Maybe they could stay in a hotel nearby—so as not to force Norrie from her room. That would be a strong enough reason. They could still spend all the time he wanted with Allessandros and Megan.

"It's no big deal. Besides, I'm staying with Stephie tonight. She's my best friend."

"We'll leave you alone. Come out when you're ready," Megan said, taking her daughter's arm and pulling her into the hall. I'll fix something cold to drink."

"Thanks, I won't be long," Gemma said, still standing near the door.

She heard the men's voices. Were they still outside?

How could she get Nikos alone? Before she could plan a way, he walked into the bedroom carrying their small suitcases.

Gemma moved swiftly, closing the door and leaning against it.

"Nikos, we can't stay here."

He calmly put the cases on the floor near the bed and surveyed the room.

"Is there a problem?"

"Look at that bed."

No, that wasn't what she wanted to say. She cleared her throat.

"I mean, this is Norrie's room. She's having to sleep at a friend's while we're here. If we stayed at a hotel, she wouldn't be forced to give up her room."

"Stay at a hotel?"

"Yes. We could book a room nearby. Still see all you want

of Allessandros and Megan and then…"

Her voice trailed off at his expression.

"I'd never offend my cousin in such a way," Nikos said firmly.

"Offend?"

"Throw his hospitality back in his face."

She took a breath to counter his argument, then slowly let it out. Leaving for a hotel would smack of rejecting their hospitality. Nervously, she glanced at the bed again.

"That's a small bed."

"If you are worried about falling out in the night, I'll hold you to make sure that doesn't happen."

Visions of being wrapped in Nikos' arms did nothing to quell the trepidation she felt. They only exacerbated the tingling sense of anticipation.

"No, I won't fall out." Or if she did, she'd just stay on the floor, where she'd be safe from temptation.

How could she tell him she wasn't worried about him being there, but about her reaction to him?

Obviously, she could never even hint at such a thing.

Maybe she could stay up all night. Or maybe between now and bedtime, she would lose the fascination she had for Nikos. Stop being so aware of his every movement, become more comfortable around him.

Comfortable? She felt as if she were on tenterhooks all the time.

Twenty minutes later, Gemma sat on the patio behind the

house with Megan and Norrie. Two-year-old Sam toddled around the grassy yard, chasing after a ball his older sister kept throwing. The two men had gone off somewhere.

Sipping the fruit punch Megan had prepared, Gemma tried to relax. There was nothing she could do about the sleeping arrangements but make the best of them. And try to get to bed before Nikos.

They'd agreed to a platonic marriage. Except for a few kisses, he had given her no sign he wanted to change that. And she fully remembered his scathing denunciation of his ex-wife. Gemma needed to prove to Nikos that he could trust her. Trust her to abide by the rules of their unconventional marriage.

"Sam's adorable," she said, watching the toddler's antics. Again, she thought about her own baby. Would she have a little boy who'd always be exploring and taking chances? Or maybe a daughter with whom she could share so much. Megan and Norrie seemed very close.

"Thanks. He's his dad all over."

"Like me?" Norrie asked.

"Yes, just like you. Both of you have Allessandros' stubborn streak."

Gemma was puzzled. Hadn't Nikos said Megan and Allessandros were married only four years ago?

"You're not exactly a marshmallow yourself, Mom," Norrie teased.

"But it gets weary standing up for myself all the time."

Norrie laughed.

"Like you don't have Daddy wrapped around your little finger."

"He's a totally frustrating, domineering, *infuriating* man."

"And here I was going to ask you for advice on dealing with Nikos," Gemma said.

"Let me guess—he's dictatorial, demanding and expects everyone to do his bidding without complaint," Megan said, her eyes dancing with amusement.

"You have known him for a long time."

Megan laughed softly.

"No, but he is very like Allessandros. Unless I stand up to him."

"That's why we don't always share exactly how our day goes. To keep Daddy from stepping in where he's really not needed."

Megan made a mock expression of horror and looked around as if searching for her husband.

"Shh, don't give away our secrets."

Norrie giggled and explained to Gemma, "It's really different in Greece. There're things I like, such as our home. It's huge and right on the water. I have a super room with a balcony. It even has stairs that lead to the garden. And we have tons of servants. I wouldn't even have to make my bed, except Mom makes me most days. Which our maid, Alyia, thinks is totally wrong."

"To be sure you know how. And Alyia knows how I feel," Megan interposed.

"Yeah, like I need to learn that."

"An old argument," Megan told Gemma.

"And then we come here and do everything ourselves," Norrie continued. "But living there is different."

"Tell me about Greece," Gemma said.

If the negotiations had not been so critical, would Nikos have agreed to his father's request and returned home to introduce his new bride?

The descriptions of the village outside of Athens that Megan and Norrie shared were like those Nikos had given her. It sounded like paradise. She'd love to go to the beach every day.

"Sometimes we visit Grandmère in France where she lives now that her husband is gone. And we spend most of the year here," Norrie finished.

"I doubt you'll live there," Megan said. "Nikos seems quite dedicated to the shipping lines, and from what Allessandros has said, he enjoys living in New York."

"We've never talked about going to Greece," Gemma said.

Of course not. Theirs was a marriage of convenience that could end at any time. There was no reason for Gemma to ever visit the Mediterranean country.

As she sat in the shade of a huge old tree talking quietly

with Allessandros's wife, Gemma suddenly knew she never wanted to end their marriage. She wanted Nikos on whatever terms he set. Lopsided marriage or not, she loved him.

He'd scoff if she ever told him. Hadn't she married him to save face? To avoid becoming an unwed mother? He'd never believe she'd fallen in love. Cynical and distrusting, Nikos would forever question her motives if she confessed her love. Better to keep it a deep secret. Even if it meant leaving as originally planned, she didn't want to give him cause to ever doubt her.

Dinner was entertaining. Gemma laughed at the constant teasing between Allessandros and Megan, and noted some similarities to the ways she'd challenged Nikos the past week. He watched the banter quietly, occasionally meeting her gaze, as if trying to divine her thoughts on the situation.

Norrie went to her friend's house right after they ate, leaving the adults in the living room with coffee. Gemma tried to enjoy the evening, but the closer the time came to go to bed, the more nervous she became.

Stop it, she chided herself. Nikos had never exceeded the bounds of propriety, and she wouldn't, either.

But it was the yearning that had her wanting more that made her nervous.

She tried to focus on the conversation, something about Nikos getting a house in Greece now that he was married again. But the words drifted by as her thoughts churned.

What would it be like to see the house Nikos grew up in, to meet his parents?

Would his father be furious he'd married another foreigner? His first marriage hadn't been a success. Did he dare admit this one wasn't, either?

"Gemma?"

She looked at Megan. "Yes?"

"You haven't heard a word we've said. Are you tired? Would you like to go to bed? Don't stay up with us if you need to get some rest. I'm always so tired during the first few months of being pregnant. We'd all understand."

Gemma sat up, snatching the excuse like a lifeline.

"I am tired."

Nikos rose as well.

"We have tomorrow to continue our visit. I'll go with Gemma."

"Oh, you don't have to. I'm tired, so I will probably go right to sleep. Stay and visit with your cousin. I'll be fine. Really."

The amusement in his eyes told him her statement didn't fool him.

"I'm tired after the hectic week we spent," he said. "Being married can wear a man out."

She grew warm as Allessandros and Megan exchanged smiles. Head held high, she bid them goodnight and headed for their room.

When the door was closed behind them, she rounded on Nikos.

"Do you know what they thought after that statement?"

He unbuttoned the top button on his dress shirt. Pausing, he looked at her.

"Who?"

"Allessandros and Megan. Saying being married can wear a man out—they probably think we've been making love all night, every night, so you can't get any sleep."

He nodded and continued to unbutton his shirt. Gemma watched as more and more of his chest was revealed. Her heart rate sped up, and her breathing grew shallow. He was a beautiful man, strong, sleek, male.

And she was in love with him.

How would it feel to touch that bronzed skin, feel the heat, run her fingertips over the contours, to let her lips and tongue taste him, caress him?

She spun around, then felt stupid staring at the door.

"I need the bathroom," she said, and almost ran from the room.

"You are acting eight, not twenty-eight," she admonished herself when alone.

Splashing water on her face, she quickly brushed her teeth and drew a deep breath. Another. Gradually, her rioting senses calmed.

"I can do this," she told her reflection.

She could go into that room, get ready for bed while Nikos used the bathroom and get in the bed. They'd already proved it was possible to sleep and nothing else. She'd turn her back on him, make sure her hands stayed firmly away from his tantalizing skin and go right to sleep.

Feigning sleep when Nikos returned to the room a few minutes after she'd dashed off her clothes and jumped beneath the covers didn't fool him for an instant. Resolutely, she kept her eyes tightly shut, her hands in fists.

He switched off the lights and climbed into his side of the bed.

She wondered if she could breathe.

"Do you like Megan?" he asked, making no effort to be quiet.

Gemma debated for a moment whether or not to answer. But he knew she wasn't asleep.

"Yes. She and I hit it off instantly. Sometimes that happens."

"They didn't have a simple time of it," he said, moving, settling in.

Gemma froze. What was he doing? The mattress moved again, and she felt the warmth of his leg beside her. Scant inches separated them. How could she be expected to sleep with him so tantalizingly close?

"What do you mean?" she asked.

Talking would be good. She could concentrate on Nikos'

deep tones and maybe fall asleep that way.

Though she instantly felt wide awake and not the least bit sleepy.

"They were sweethearts during college, then had a big fight. Neither can remember what it was about, but they went their separate ways. Neither he nor Megan knew she was pregnant."

"So they did just get married four years ago," she murmured.

"He was on an assignment to the United States and ran into her at an art gallery featuring a new artist. They'd been lovers in college. For ten years, she'd thought he'd abandoned her. And when he found her again, he told her he thought she'd run away with another man. It's hard to rebuild trust once it's been shattered."

"They seem perfect for each other. And both children are precious."

"I want to discuss something with you," Nikos said, slipping his arm beneath her neck and slowly drawing her closer.

Instantly, heat cascaded through Gemma. She could hardly breathe. How could she talk? His body was hard against the softer curves of her own. His scent seemed to invade every cell. Bracing herself, she found her hand pushed against his chest. She could feel the slow, steady beat of his heart. Her fingers curled slightly, feeling the strength of his chest.

"What?"

One word. If she could say one word, she could say more. At least she hoped so.

Right now, all she could do was concentrate on the sensations that swept through her. His arm beneath her neck, her head resting against his shoulder. The heat beneath the sheet that enveloped them both. His steady pulse felt steady against her fingertips while hers was racing.

"You and me. So far, only the two of us and your friend Susan know the true circumstances of our marriage. I want our situation to stay that way. At least until I see my father. I've told him what he needs to know at this stage."

"You didn't tell Allessandros?"

"No. He may have guessed. I'll tell my parents when we see them. That could be months from now, depending on how soon I get permanent residence status. By then, I expect we'll have resolved our future."

She drew another shaky breath. By the time he returned home to visit, their marriage could be over.

Except she didn't want it to be over.

But what did Nikos want?

Chapter Eight

Nikos felt Gemma's hand on his chest and everything inside him tightened. It was dark, quiet. He was alone in bed with a woman who was his wife. They had agreed to a platonic relationship, which had suited him when they made their unlikely bargain.

Now, however, he wanted to change the rules. Holding an armful of sweet femininity and doing nothing was almost more than a red-blooded man could tolerate. He wanted to bury himself in her, taste the sweet honey of her mouth, feel her satiny skin warm to his touch. Hear her soft cries of pleasure as they explored the heights of passion together.

But would Gemma join him in that exploration?

Or run screaming from the room?

If she remained, she'd probably expect some declaration of love. Wasn't that something all women wanted? Even if it was only said in the heat of passion?

And that he couldn't say.

He didn't believe in the emotion. It was simply words women used to cover up the baser instincts such as greed and self-serving manipulation.

He'd thought he'd found love with Katrina, only to discover the woman he'd believed she was, never existed. Learning from that, Nikos knew women wanted to bind men in the throes of passion in order to get what they wanted—material things, power or prestige.

What did Gemma want?

To be the strongest in a negotiation, a man needed to know what his opposition's goals were. What was important, what was not.

The key with Gemma would be her baby.

Feeling her fingers flex against his chest almost clouded his mind enough to forget where he was. He grasped her hand, clasping it in his to keep her from distracting him.

"If we continue as we have this past week, I see no reason to end this marriage once the green card is issued. We deal well together. And with Hal to help, you could continue to work after your baby is born, if you wished. Or stay home," he said, testing the waters.

She was silent. He wondered what thoughts milled around in her mind. She constantly surprised him. Was it because she'd been on her own so long she didn't react as he expected women to do?

Or was she just cleverer than Katrina had been?

"I know you're not asleep. If my suggestion is too abhorrent to consider, just say so."

He hadn't expected to feel impatient, frustrated that she hadn't instantly jumped at the opportunity to remain in the marriage.

"No, no, Nikos, it's not abhorrent at all. You caught me by surprise. I mean, why me?"

"Why you what?"

"You could marry anyone in the world. Why settle for me?"

"First, I cannot marry anyone else right now—I'm already married. And second, I'm not settling for anyone. We've worked well together professionally for years. I think we can forge a strong partnership in our personal lives as well."

She didn't answer immediately.

His impatience grew. His suggestion didn't need that much consideration. She should know by now if she wanted to stay married or not. It wasn't as if she had other alternatives. Should he remind her of that?

"If you are worried about your baby, I'll be as good a father as I can for the child."

"But the baby isn't yours."

He was silent. Did she think he couldn't grow to care for a child merely because it wasn't his? The child was hers. He liked her. Ergo, he could grow to like the child.

"I care for Norrie and Sam. They're not mine."

"I meant, wouldn't you like a child of your own?"

"Are you offering?"

Silence again.

He frowned into the night, wishing she'd open that sassy mouth and tell him what she thought and what she thought he should think, as she'd done several nights last week. Maybe he should make it an order, rile her up to force an honest reaction.

"Gemma, that's not something you have to decide right now. It's a moot point for several months. We can reevaluate the situation later. The issue at hand is whether or not to continue this marriage."

"I enjoy being married to you," she said so softly he almost missed the words.

But he heard them. And the depth of feeling that settled over him was unexpected.

"However, I'm not sure we suit," she added.

"You suit me fine. You're undemanding, are not grasping and greedy, and still have one of the finest business minds I deal with."

"Gee, how romantic."

"Romance doesn't play a part in this. We'd go on as we started."

"Very well, Nikos. If you're sure."

Despite her words, he heard the hesitation, the uncertainty. Time would prove him right. They would have a stable business marriage. And tied to him legally, she couldn't leave. He'd keep his personal assistant and continue building

ALK Shipping until it was the largest shipping line in the world.

Normally, the completing of a deal called for a handshake. But Nikos had no intention of shaking his wife's hand. Instead, he pulled her up across his chest and kissed her, threading his fingers into her soft bouncy curls, relishing the sensations that exploded through his body.

Her mouth opened to his, enticing him with its honey-hot sweetness. Her hands delved into his hair and caressed him, while one silky leg slipped between his. He wanted more, but it was too soon.

Lust grew, passion built. But, afraid to alarm her, he eased off. He planned to do his seduction of her slowly. Until he had her bound to him in all the ways he could devise, he wanted nothing to scare her off.

Gemma differed from Katrina. Special. And someone he could envision living with until he grew old.

But with his blood thundering through his veins, he was hard-pressed to muster the control necessary to slow down tonight. One hand swept across her back, feeling her muscles move beneath her cotton gown. Unable to resist, he filled his palm with the softness of her bottom. He wanted more, wanted to delve into the heat at her core, to take all the ardor she possessed and lavish it on himself.

With monumental effort, he moved his hand. Brought their kiss to an end.

Pleased to know she was breathing as hard as if she'd run a race, Nikos had to satisfy himself with that. Progress sometimes came one step at a time.

"When we return to New York, we'll have to shop for baby furniture," he said.

A safe topic, one guaranteed to cool his hunger.

It wasn't what he wanted to talk about. He wanted to talk about making love to his wife. But not until she was ready.

And he needed to make sure of her before moving to the next step.

His mouth continued to hunger for the taste of hers. His control was sorely tested as he gazed into the blackness and willed himself to keep his arm from tightening, to keep from throwing everything to the wind and making love to her all night long.

Gemma was more confused than ever when they returned home on Sunday. Standing at the large window in the living room of their apartment, she gazed out at the darkness. It was after ten, and she was alone, except for Hal, who was in his quarters.

The weekend had gone well. Allessandros seemed pleased his cousin had married. Megan welcomed her warmly. And she'd loved Norrie and Sam. It was the thought of their deception that still lay heavily on her.

That and the abandonment of her husband.

Nikos had dropped her off on their return to New York that afternoon and headed for the office. Negotiations resumed in the morning and he wanted to review some critical files.

Or at least that was what he told her.

Not that she didn't believe him, but he could have reviewed them early in the morning. If he needed to at all. His mind never seemed to forget a single fact. What did he need to examine now?

She noticed her reflection in the glass. Her hair waved around her face, softening her features. Her figure was still slim, showing only the slightest hint of the changes to come.

He had said last night he wanted to extend their marriage. She knew she hadn't dreamed that.

Had she?

Turning, she wandered over to the sofa and sank down beside the book she'd brought to read. As if her mind could concentrate on anything.

Nikos had treated her almost like a mere acquaintance today.

She'd expected on waking this morning to find a new closeness between them. Something to show they'd be able to forge a strong bond that would bind them together through the years. A suggestion that he looked on her as more than only a personal assistant he didn't wish to lose.

Careful not to give any sign of the love that threatened to overwhelm her, she was content to take tiny steps forward until Nikos might grow comfortable with their change of status.

Instead, he'd been cool, polite and distant.

Except for the blazing memories of his kisses, of the sensations she experienced when his hands caressed her as she rested against his muscular chest, she might have thought she imagined last night.

Was this his way of advancing their marriage? One step forward, two back?

What did he want from her?

"Probably a barrier between him and all the women who chase him," she muttered, frowning. Jumping to her feet, she paced to the window again.

"I could have gone to the office with him," she said to her reflection.

"Indeed you could have," Nikos said from the doorway.

She spun around.

"In fact, I should have had you join me. I had the devil's own time finding some of the cargo manifests I wanted to use as examples."

"They're in a file in Elise's area," she said, finding it difficult to switch into efficient assistant mode when her recent thoughts had nothing to do with business.

"I located them. I wish to leave early in the morning. If

you can't be ready, I'll have Hal return to pick you up."

"I can be ready as early as you like."

If nothing else, she prided herself on her professionalism and devotion to her job. She was good at it, as he well knew.

How could she make herself equally indispensable in his personal life?

He glanced at his watch.

Stubbornly refusing to take the bait, Gemma remained silent, watching. Feasting on him with her eyes. He looked tired. The lines around his eyes suggested strain.

She shouldn't be surprised. The negotiations were a tremendous responsibility. If they could get their terms, or close to them, it would make a monumental difference to their rate structures. Which would lead to more business. Expansion was the name of the game, and he was looking to increase revenues with the recent acquisition of the Alteras Company.

She wished she could offer assurance that everything would turn out the way he wanted.

She almost laughed. He certainly didn't need platitudes from a personal assistant.

Or a wife.

"I'll see you in the morning, then," he said.

Gemma hesitated, almost ready to confront him, but then shrugged. It was as clear a dismissal as she'd ever heard.

Feeling hurt he hadn't wanted to spend some time with

her, she went straight to her room.

Eyeing the connecting door as she prepared for bed, she wished she still shared the room with him.

What if the INS required a second inspection? Should she raise that point with him? Would he suggest they share a bed to answer any questions again?

No. He'd compared her to Katrina and other women. They all wanted something from him. If she was to pique his interest, she'd better remember that.

Dressing slowly for bed, she tried to envision herself as some fascinating creature who could captivate any man. Maybe because it was so late, but she had difficulty imagining herself as interesting. And in a few months, she'd be a blimp. No one would find her attractive then. Probably not even a devoted husband—which Nikos definitely was not.

She wanted his respect, attention—love.

"Might as well wish for a million dollars," she mused, climbing into her lonely bed. "It's as likely to appear as it would be to have him fall wildly in love with me."

The next week passed at a frantic pace. The meetings with Frank LeBec went on day after day, well into the evening hours. Repeatedly Gemma thought the end was in sight, only to have Nikos balk at a demand or Frank refuse a point. She was kept busy verifying data and statistics, pulling up examples and extrapolating what different compromises would entail.

Whenever they took a break, Nikos would close the two of them in his office and rehash the points they'd made or speculate on what the next counter demand would be. It was exhilarating, but hectic.

By Thursday, she was exhausted. And wondering when the contract would be finalized—if ever. The current one expired soon. While the shipping company could fall back on the same standard longshoreman's contract as negotiated with all other shipping lines, Nikos still wanted better terms.

Gemma sat at the negotiating table watching Nikos, trying to anticipate what he might need to shore up a point or add strength to their bid. But more and more, as the week went on, she slipped into daydreams.

Had she imagined their night in Washington? Had he really said he wanted their marriage to continue? Would they ever grow close enough to share thoughts and dreams?

Or would he always remain distant? A business arrangement that suited him and made her feel alone and left out?

If the pace of the week was a sign, time would pass swiftly being married to Nikos, but somehow it wasn't the relationship she'd longed for in a marriage.

She wanted the evenings back the way they were during their first week together. Quietly sitting together on the sofa, gazing at the stunning view. Talking, exploring each other's past. Building routines that'd see them through the years.

She even missed Hal's cooking. A hasty bagel in the morning was the extent of breakfast. Lunches and dinners were catered in the conference room. And she was too tired when she returned to the apartment each night to do anything but fall into bed.

She was getting cranky. She was so tired. Groaning softly, she wondered when she could escape. Why did Nikos drag the meetings on? LeBec was becoming truculent.

Maybe she could suggest an early day tomorrow and let things simmer over the weekend. Returning fresh Monday morning might be a plan beneficial to both sides. Or they could realize they'd reached an impasse and do something to kick it loose.

Looking around the table, she realized the men were looking at her expectantly.

What had she missed?

"Gemma, you started to say something?" Nikos said.

Making up her mind, she decided to act. One way or another, she needed to get out of the room.

"Actually, I'd like to take a brief break and speak with you, Nikos, if you don't mind."

The men rose as she did and she nodded at their manners, sweeping out of the conference room and into Nikos' office. He followed moments later.

"Yes?"

His tone was cool, his manner guarded.

"I'm tired. I'm going home. But before I do, I want you to know I think you should sign the agreement as stated an hour ago. I don't think LeBec is going to budge any further. And it incorporates almost everything you want. Twice you've put his back up, and sometimes pride is all-important to some men. Even at the risk of losing advantages in a business deal."

He studied her gravely.

"I don't think I need you to make my business decisions for me."

"I'm not making any decisions, just offering some advice. Another piece of advice—take a break. Reconvene on Monday. That'll give everyone time to really think through the points on the table."

She rubbed her forehead, wishing she was already in her bed.

"Are you ill?"

Immediately concerned, Nikos stepped closer and rested his hands on her shoulders.

At the warm touch, Gemma was hard-pressed not to give in and lean into his strength. She'd love nothing better than to be enveloped in his arms, to rest her head against his shoulder and let him take over.

"I'm fine," she replied, standing straight and gently shrugging off his hands. "Just tired. I have a headache. You don't need me at the table. I want to go home."

"I'll take you."

"No. You go back and finish arguing with LeBec."

"Sit. I'll call Hal."

He guided her to a chair. Crossing to the desk, he punched in a number. In only seconds, he instructed Hal to bring the car. Calling Elise, he asked her to come into the office.

"She'll stay with you until Hal arrives," Nikos said as he lowered the receiver.

"I'm not sick, just tired."

But Gemma's protest was halfhearted. She enjoyed being cosseted.

Elise was concerned when she hurried into the office.

"Are you all right? Nothing wrong with the baby, is there?" she asked, crossing immediately to Gemma.

Both Nikos and Gemma looked at her in stunned surprise.

"What? It's not a secret, is it?" Elise asked, seeing their expressions. "Honestly," she said in exasperation, her hands on her hips. "I had five girls and three of them have had babies. Think I don't know the signs?"

"There's nothing wrong with anything except I've got a bit of a headache and am tired," Gemma said.

"Not surprising—you've been pushing too hard this week."

Elise rounded on Nikos. "You should take better care of her."

"Hal will be here in a short time. If I'm still tied up, will you walk her to the car?"

His even tone didn't hide his displeasure at her tone.

"Nikos. I'm fine," Gemma protested.

Cosseting was one thing. Being treated like an invalid was another.

"Allow me to care for my wife in the manner I think best," he said arrogantly.

She almost groaned at his tone, but only nodded and closed her eyes. It felt good to just sit for a moment and do nothing. As soon as she got home, she'd take a nap and when she awoke, she'd feel right as rain.

"Gemma?"

Nikos' voice woke her.

"What?"

He leaned over her, shaking her shoulder gently.

"You fell asleep. Hal's here with the car. Let's get you home."

Elise was no longer in the office.

"Okay."

She experienced a slight feeling of disorientation. She'd planned to wait until she arrived home to fall asleep. It seemed she was more exhausted than she thought.

Nikos put his arm around her waist and walked with her to the door.

"I can manage," she said.

The last thing she wanted was to take Nikos away from the negotiations.

"I'm sure you can. Indulge me."

Elise's sympathetic gaze met hers as they walked through her office.

"I hope you feel better, Gemma."

"Thanks."

Gemma felt as if the eyes of every employee were on them as Nikos solicitously matched her steps to the elevator.

"Shouldn't you be in the conference room?" she asked crankily.

So much fuss embarrassed her.

"I did as you suggested and agreed to the terms. Phil and his staff are finalizing the documents. Once LeBec reviews them to make sure we don't pull a fast one, as he said, then he'll present it to their membership. With any luck, we'll have our agreement signed by all parties as early as next Wednesday. Two days before the current contract expires."

His response took aback Gemma. He'd agreed to the contract as she'd suggested?

"You surprise me. I thought you wanted to get him to accept all your terms. I thought for sure the negotiations would go on and on."

The elevator reached the lobby, and Nikos walked her to the double glass doors. She saw Nikos' car double-parked in front.

"I'll be fine from here," she said.

"I'm going home with you," Nikos said as he nodded to Hal and opened the back door.

"What?" Gemma swung around and stared at him. "I'm not sick, Nikos."

"Neither are you up to your normal, healthy stamina. Permit a husband to indulge himself and take care of his wife."

His statement almost made her smile.

"Thank you. But I really just want to go home and lie down for a nap. I'll be fine once I wake up, you'll see."

"Then, by all means, let's be on our way."

Gemma dozed in the car. When they arrived at the apartment, she stumbled when getting out, glad of Nikos' arm, which immediately caught her. Without another word, he swept her up into his arms and strode into the building. The doorman opened the door with alacrity.

"Is madam all right?" he asked solicitously.

"She will be soon," Nikos said, striding to the elevators.

"Put me down," Gemma hissed, even as her arm came around his neck.

"When we reach our floor. I can't have you collapsing on me."

"I can walk—I just tripped."

The elevator whisked them to their floor in only seconds. Nikos seemed content to hold her, ignoring her requests to put her on her feet.

Gemma was secretly thrilled he even thought to carry her. No one had done that since she'd been a baby. And if only she felt better, she knew she'd have cherished the experience.

Could she get him to do it again when she felt better?

Heat stole into her cheeks at the very thought, so Gemma gave up and leaned her head against his shoulder. She could almost fall asleep in his arms.

Like she had in Washington.

Nikos walked into her room and gently set her on the bed.

"Slip out of those things and get into something more comfortable," he suggested.

"I will."

She closed her eyes and drifted to the left until she fell back against the mattress. It felt so good to lie down. She'd change her clothes in just a second.

"Gemma?"

"Mmm."

If she didn't have to open her eyes, she'd be all right. Even her face hurt, she was so tired.

"I'll help you."

Gemma tried to sit up when he tugged gently on her arm. Two minutes later, her eyes snapped open. He'd removed her suit jacket and was unbuttoning her blouse. She slapped at his hands.

"I can manage."

"I doubt it."

The material parted as he swept it off her shoulders.

"Where's your nightgown?"

"Under the pillow," she said, suddenly wide awake.

Conscious of how scantily attired she was, she snatched at the white gown when he pulled it out and held it against her chest.

"I can manage the rest," she said breathlessly.

"With the two of us working together, you can be in bed in seconds," he said, already reaching to unfasten her skirt.

Gemma tried to slap away his hand again, but he was already sliding the material over her hips.

"Step out," he ordered, pulling her gently to her feet which allowed the skirt to puddle at her feet.

Nikos then reached up to peel off her panty hose.

"Nikos, stop," she said.

If he didn't stop soon, she'd make a huge mistake and throw herself into his arms.

He slowly rose, his gaze roaming over her until he met her eyes. Slowly, he smiled, and Gemma almost sank back on the bed. Her knees definitely didn't work well under that look.

"I never expected my business-focused personal assistant to indulge herself in such provocative underwear."

Reaching out a hand, he ran a fingertip along the top of the lacy edge of her bra, outlining the swell of her breasts.

She was acutely conscious of how scantily attired she was.

The brief bikini panties and lacy bra were an indulgence, just as he said. One she had felt safe in luxuriating in because no one else would ever know. Or so she'd thought.

He leaned over and kissed her.

Forgetting everything, she dropped the nightgown and reached up to encircle his neck. His hands were warm and firm against her back as he pressed her against him. She could feel the rough material of his suit, the heat of his body igniting heat in her own. He brought her to life, exhaustion forgotten, as his touch built a craving that had yet to be assuaged.

He pulled back and gazed into her eyes. She almost forgot her own name at the latent desire that shone clearly in his face. They were alone in the apartment, had the rest of the day to themselves. Would he stay? Would he—

Nikos muttered something under his breath and broke the embrace, reaching down to pick up her nightgown. He slipped it over her head, reached around and unfastened her bra and drew it away.

Gemma slipped her arms through the sleeves and felt the soft cotton drift down.

"Into bed," he said, sweeping back the covers. "Now, Gemma, before I forget how tired you are and join you."

Her heart pounding in her chest, she looked into his eyes. She longed to invite him to do just that, but dared she?

Before she could say anything, he'd crossed the room to the door. Gemma pulled back the covers and slipped beneath them. Closing her eyes, she turned on her side, away from Nikos, away from the embarrassment of practically throwing herself at him. Such desire had to result from raging hormones from the pregnancy.

If he said anything about it, she'd excuse it with that.

"Gemma," he called softly.

"Mmm?" The brief flash of energy had dissipated. She was almost asleep.

"Another time I won't leave."

Chapter Nine

It was dark when Gemma awoke. She lay in bed for a long moment thinking. Had Nikos said what she thought he'd said just before she fell asleep?

Impossible.

She rose and went to wash her face. Donning a light robe, she wandered out to the living room. Soft lighting illuminated the room. Nikos lay on the sofa. She paused in the shadows of the hallway for a long moment, watching him. He was reading a book, and the scene looked infinitely dear to her.

She must have made some movement or noise, because he suddenly looked right at her.

Rising swiftly, he crossed the room.

"Are you feeling better?" he asked, raising her chin with his finger to look into her eyes.

"Yes, thank you. I'm sorry to flake out on you like that."

"We've had a hectic week. Come on, I'll have Hal prepare you something to eat."

"How late is it?" she asked as they walked to the dining room.

"A bit after ten."

"He'll have retired. Don't bother him. I can scrounge something to eat in the kitchen."

"He's still up and has been waiting for you to awaken. I believe he's prepared something especially for you."

Ten minutes later, Gemma sat at the dining table with a large bowl of chicken noodle soup and warm rolls in front of her.

"Is this some kind of universal remedy?" she asked as she dipped her spoon into the bowl.

Hal stood near the doorway watching closely. Nikos sat in his chair, watching her closely .

"Mmm, it's delicious."

She smiled at Hal and inclined her head in the same manner Nikos often did. "Thank you, Hal. It's perfect."

He bowed and left, but she glimpsed the pleased look in his eyes.

"You have a loyal servant for life," Nikos said casually. "Tell me the significance of chicken noodle soup."

Gemma smiled and ate some more. The warm rolls Hal prepared went well with the soup.

"It's supposed to make you feel better if you're sick. I'm not sick, just tired, but it's making me feel better. I take it you don't have such a thing in Greece?"

Slowly, he shook his head.

"Sometimes when I was a boy and sick, my mother

prepared a broth but no noodles. If I become sick, you'll have to remind me to try this."

She nodded, unable to imagine the man ever falling victim to any illness. He'd never had as much as a cold in all the years she'd known him.

"Should you consider cutting back at work?" Nikos asked.

Gemma looked up.

"No. I'm not sick, Nikos, just pregnant. This week has been hectic and the hours long. But I can manage a normal workweek. I can do my job."

"We'll see how you feel on Monday."

"I'll feel fine."

He smiled at her certainty and she felt that flutter in her heart again.

"If you're feeling rested in the morning, I thought we'd go shopping for baby furniture."

She tilted her head to the side.

"I can't picture you shopping for furniture."

"How do you think I get new pieces?"

"Wave a hand and order some interior designer to go buy it?"

"And I thought you were an astute businesswoman. I picked out almost every stick of furniture in this apartment. I kept nothing from Katrina's time."

"I stand corrected. But don't you think it's a bit early to be buying furniture for the baby? I'm not due for almost five months."

"I realize that, but this is a good time. The negotiations are complete. We have a few days before we leave, so why not now?"

"Leave? Leave for where?"

"Phil contacted me this afternoon. My petition for permanent residence was approved. The marriage made the difference. I can now travel outside the US and get back in with no trouble."

"Oh, that was fast."

"I thought so as well. Phil said I should have the final documents early next week."

"And now you want to leave?"

"To visit Greece. I phoned my father this afternoon to let him know the negotiations were accomplished as we wanted. And to tell him I remarried. He and my mother want to meet you. Allessandros already told him about you and he insists we visit. I told him we'd leave as soon as the contracts were signed. As long as your doctor says traveling will pose no danger to you. It's a long journey."

She put down her spoon, butterflies suddenly dancing in her stomach.

"I don't think I should go," she said. "I'm not sure your parents are going to be thrilled with me as a new daughter-in-law, even a temporary one. Maybe you should explain things to them and…"

She let her words trail off at the frown on his face.

"Of course you should go. They'll love you. And we don't need to talk at all about our reasons for marriage. I thought if we get everything wound up by the end of the week, we could leave next Friday."

She opened her mouth to protest, then closed it abruptly. That look was familiar to her. Her bossy husband would not budge on this issue.

And she couldn't help feeling some anticipation to see where Nikos grew up, to meet more of his family. It made this fake marriage seem even more real.

Though, maybe it wasn't such a fake marriage after all. He had his green card and never said a word about ending things. What he'd suggested in Washington echoed.

The next morning, Gemma awoke refreshed. The long nap and a solid night's sleep had done wonders.

She showered and dressed quickly, trying on several outfits until she settled on a loose cotton sundress. Her jeans no longer fit comfortably. Brushing her hair, she was pleased to note the circles beneath her eyes were gone. Healthy color glowed in her cheeks.

Nikos was already at the dining room table, the remnants of his breakfast in front of him as he sipped coffee and read some papers.

How domestic, she thought as she slipped into her seat. She wished she felt more comfortable in the situation.

"Good morning," he said. "You look much better."

"I feel wonderful."

"Up to shopping, then?"

"Always," she replied as Hal entered, carrying a fresh pot of tea.

"Have you decided which room to use as a nursery?" Nikos asked.

For a moment Gemma wanted to tell him she wanted to use *her* room, as it was next to his. But then he'd wonder where she planned to stay, and somehow she hadn't figured out a way to get him to invite her back into his room, to insist she share that big bed.

She nodded. "Initially, the baby can bunk in with me. Then I thought the yellow room across the hall."

Nikos nodded, saying nothing.

What was he thinking, she wondered. How was it possible she anticipated his needs in business so easily and yet had no clue about what he thought when they were home?

When she had finished eating, Nikos instructed Hal to have the car available in thirty minutes.

As they wandered around the infant department in a large store an hour later, Gemma realized for the first time what a difference a baby would make in her life. She felt suddenly grateful for the magnitude of Nikos' gesture in marrying her.

She appreciated the fact she wouldn't have to go through her pregnancy alone. That she'd have someone to share the difficulties with. Someone to be with her when the baby arrived.

Watching Nikos as he moved purposefully among the furniture, she suspected he'd prove to be a good father. He'd make sure any child felt secure and loved. And he'd teach him as well about honesty and honor.

She almost stopped in her tracks when she realized how fervently she wished the baby was his. She felt as if she was shortchanging the man who offered her so much.

"Something wrong?" he asked, as if attuned to her.

She looked up, searching for something that would let her continue on this path.

"No, except…"

He glanced at her and then took her hand, threading his fingers through hers as he pulled her out of the aisle and into a small space near the infant swings.

"What?"

She took a deep breath.

"Nikos, I don't think I can go through with this after all. I'm taking and taking, and you're getting nothing out of this arrangement."

"Buying baby furniture?"

She shook her head, wanting to make him understand.

"No, not that. This marriage. You got your green card and can stay in the country. And with the negotiations finished…"

"There's the Alteras merger to incorporate, don't forget."

"I know, but to be stuck with me and with James's baby…"

She ran out of words, feeling miserable.

"Ah, I think I see where you are going with this. Do you still long for James?"

"No! He's despicable. I'd never take up with the man again, knowing what I know now. I feel sorry for his wife and sorry for him and all the joy he'll miss not knowing this baby. But I never want to have anything to do with him."

Her sincerity rang clearly.

"I loved him once, but he destroyed that love forever. And turned out to be a completely different man from what I thought he was."

"Then I cannot see the problem."

"It's not fair to you."

For a long moment Nikos stared at her.

"How is it unfair?"

"You should have someone fresh and free from complications from a previous relationship. Someone who knows how to dress for high society and fit in with galas and opening nights. Someone who will give you lots of babies."

"And you can't?"

She blinked. "I don't know."

She was silent for a moment, thinking.

"The event we went to wasn't the disaster I expected."

"I was speaking of lots of babies."

"Oh."

Heat swept through her as she thought of having Nikos'

babies. Of dark-haired infants with black eyes.

Her heart rate soared.

"Of course I could, if you really wanted. But after the night at Allessandros and Megan's, you said nothing more. I thought you'd changed your mind."

He raised their linked hands, turning so he could brush his lips across the back of hers.

"I did not change my mind."

He looked at her with grave eyes.

"If you had been married before with a child and your husband had died or you divorced him, would you expect never to get married again?"

She shook her head.

"Nor would I. If Katrina and I had had a child, and it lived with me, would you come to care for that child?"

"I think I would."

"That's what I think about your baby. I believe I'll grow to care for that baby as if he or she were my own. Another man may have sired the child, but I will be its father."

Tears welled in her eyes, and she tried to absorb the full extent of his statement.

"Thank you," she whispered, tightening her grip on his hand.

He brushed back some of her hair, his fingers lingering against her cheek.

"Let us have no more doubts, all right?"

She nodded, love overflowing for this powerful man. If she hadn't already tumbled in love with him, this would have caused her to do so. Now his comment strengthened her feelings. But she knew better than to allow a hint of that love to show.

That had not been part of their bargain.

"Then let's go find the best crib we can for our baby," she said calmly.

They examined every crib and listened to the salesclerk explain the various safety features, the benefits of one over another. Gemma was pleased to discover she and Nikos both liked the same one, in cherry wood with carved spindles. They bought a matching cradle and a changing table. Then a whimsical mobile—Nikos' idea.

Browsing through the bedding, they selected colorful sheets and blankets.

"We should buy some clothes, too," Nikos said.

"Not that the baby will need much," she murmured as she piled the bedding in Nikos' arms.

"You may find things in Greece you'd like to get, too," Nikos said.

"Mmm."

She still had doubts and concerns about the impending visit, but she was curious to see his home, to meet his parents and learn more about her husband.

By the time they'd finished shopping, Gemma was glad to

return to the apartment. She was ready for another nap. She hoped this fatigue didn't last the entire nine months.

Entering the apartment, she instantly felt at home. What had changed? Knowing how Nikos felt toward her baby was one factor. Was hope another? Would someday her husband grow to care for her as he promised to grow to care for her child?

"If we're leaving at the end of next week, there're a bunch of loose ends to wind up. You can stay home all week and rest. And when the furniture's delivered, you can show them where to put everything."

"I'm not staying home. We can let Hal know where to put things. I'll keep the cradle in my room for the first few weeks. But we can set up the rest of the furniture in the yellow room."

"You need rest."

"I'll get enough rest, even if I have to go to bed at seven thirty. But I'm not sick or an invalid. I can do my job."

He looked frustrated.

"Very well. We'll see how the week goes."

She nodded. "And it'll go fine."

He looked at his watch. "I'm going to the office for a little while today. I'll be back before dinner."

"I could go in with you," she offered.

Nikos shook his head.

"Rest up. Time enough Monday for the hectic pace at work. Besides, I suspect you'd like to go through the things we bought."

Smiling at the thought of the layette, of the tiny baby clothes and the velvety soft teddy bear Nikos also insisted they purchase, Gemma hesitated.

"Actually I would, but I'll wait for you. We can ooh and ahh over them together."

He looked at her for a moment, then shook his head slowly.

"I'm not a man to ooh and ahh over things."

She laughed.

"Okay, then you can just hand them to me one by one, and I'll do enough for both of us."

He frowned.

She laughed softly again and reached out to pat his arm.

"Don't worry, we'll have fun together.."

"I'm sure of it. You have a knack for making the ordinary special," Nikos said.

He drew her closer and kissed her quickly, then set her free.

"I'll be home for dinner. Tell Hal."

With that, he was gone.

Grateful for the time to rest over the weekend, Gemma took advantage of every moment. She slept in late Sunday and even napped in the afternoon. By Monday, she felt refreshed and ready to face the week.

Shortly before quitting time Monday afternoon, Nikos stepped out of his office.

"Hal called—the furniture has arrived. Turns out the crib came in a box and needs assembling. I thought we could leave early and assemble the crib after dinner."

Gemma looked up, startled. He seemed as interested in getting things set up for the baby as she was.

"Assembly? The delivery guys didn't do it?"

"Apparently not."

"Do you know anything about assembling furniture?"

"No, but how hard can it be?"

"Okay. I'll just tidy my desk and be ready."

"Hal will be downstairs with the car in twenty minutes."

Once home, they changed into casual clothes and hurried through dinner. Gemma felt the excitement grow at the thought of getting the baby's room ready. As if a treat awaited, instead of an unfamiliar chore.

Gemma had chosen the yellow room across the long hall from her own. The baby monitor they'd purchased insured she'd be able to hear the baby no matter where she went in the apartment, but she liked the thought of having the child close. Once it graduated from the cradle, that is.

They'd checked out the furniture when they first arrived at home. They'd positioned the dresser against a wall and placed the changing table in front of it. The rocker set at an angle. The crib was in a big box leaning against another wall. A smaller box held the cradle.

Gemma noted that Hal had emptied the room before the delivery.

"Are you sure you want to do this?" Gemma asked, looking at the boxes yet to be opened.

"Certain."

A few minutes later, Nikos had the parts of the crib spread across the floor. It turned out to be a simple task to affix the ends, the slide rails, the sides of the crib, insert the springs. Gemma held the ends as he attached the various items.

He could almost feel her excitement.

"Did Hal wash the linen?" he asked as he tightened a screw.

"Yes, everything's ready to be used. But if we set it up this early, everything will be dusty before the baby's born."

"And everything can be washed again," he said.

She smiled at him, her eyes shining.

"Yes, that's true, isn't it? I can't wait to see how it all will look."

He stared at her for a long moment, forgetting the screwdriver he held, forgetting the last steps left in the crib's assembly. She looked so pretty holding the end of the crib, her eyes full of dreams. He wasn't expecting to feel so much for her. Their relationship had always been completely business like.

But he wanted her. Tightening his grip on the screwdriver, he drew a deep breath. When she looked up at him with that smile, he wanted to throw caution to the wind, sweep her into his arms and kiss her until tomorrow.

"We still have the cradle to assemble, too, don't forget," she said happily. "I didn't realize how multi-talented you are. This is great."

Sycophants over the years had tried flattery to get something, but the compliment from Gemma was heartfelt. And touched him as nothing else ever had.

Dragging his gaze away from her, he finished what he was doing.

"Wait a minute and you can help me make up the crib," she said, hurrying from the room.

In two minutes she was back, arms piled high with the bedding.

Nikos enjoyed working with her. His fingers brushed hers as they smoothed the sheet, brightly covered with circus animals.

"Okay, now set up the mobile," she ordered, placing the teddy bear in one corner.

Once they finished, he could escape to the office, immerse himself in the last-minute details he wanted to complete before their trip. Focus on something to take his mind off the growing desire he felt for her.

But until then, the sweet scent of his wife and her enthusiastic delight in the mundane task of making a baby's bed surrounded him.

When they entered her bedroom to assemble the cradle,

Nikos hesitated in the doorway. There was a feminine feel to the room he'd never noticed before. Her scent filled the air, a frilly nightgown lay where tossed across the pillow, trailing to the floor. Near the dresser was a pair of high heels, one on its side, as if Gemma had kicked them off and let them stay where they landed.

The need to distance himself grew. He was growing too interested in her, too involved. Too caught up in the fantasy of a family life, or what one could be like.

Yet nothing had been confirmed with a lasting commitment. Time enough to reevaluate the situation once the baby was born.

The cradle looked small when he lifted it onto the supports a few minutes later. Gently pushing it, he could picture a tiny infant snuggled down in it, soothed by the swaying.

He brought his gaze up to Gemma. Would the baby look like her?

She smiled and reached out to touch his arm.

"Thanks. This is perfect."

He drew her into the circle of his arms and lowered his face to kiss her. She tasted sweet and warm and womanly. Deepening the kiss, he let the feelings sweep through him, hot and exciting. He wanted her.

Then he stepped back, turned and left the room. That road was one he had traveled before. He didn't plan to go that way again. He needed distance. Distance and distractions. Gemma wasn't Katrina.

Even so, the better way forward was not to fall in love with his wife.

A week later, while gazing out the window on the flight to London, Gemma remembered every caress and embrace she'd shared with Nikos.

For the three days after leaving so abruptly Monday night, he hadn't touched her once.

Yet hadn't he said something about wanting to be a daddy to her baby? Didn't that imply a future together? Granted, they'd been inundated with tasks at work that took a lot of concentration and long hours. But the rides to and from were quiet. He could have brought up the topic.

Confused, she tried to find some glimmer of understanding about the complex man sitting beside her in first class. But she felt no closer than the day he'd proposed his wild scheme of a marriage of convenience.

When they returned to New York, she'd definitely give Megan a call to see if she could shed some light on how to deal with her husband. It was obvious from the love and devotion between Megan and Allessandros they'd found the key. While Gemma didn't expect love from Nikos, maybe she could at least figure out how to draw closer.

Always keeping her own love for him a secret.

He'd never mentioned expecting love in their relationship.

And after his experience with Katrina, she knew he didn't have a high opinion of love.

But it was hard to resist touching him, soaking up every scrap of time with him, listening to his every word.

From London, they flew to Athens. Spending the night in a luxurious hotel, Gemma saw little of the city; she was too tired and eager for sleep. Early the next morning, they boarded a private jet, which flew them directly to the seaside town of Pylos.

"It's beautiful," she exclaimed as the plane banked into a turn on its final approach to the small airport. The Ionian Sea was a deep blue with sugar white sandy shores edging it. A wide stretch of lush green bordered the beach. The white buildings below were dazzling in the sun.

"I have always thought so," Nikos said, leaning close as he, too, gazed from the window.

For him, it was home. Would she ever feel like this place was home?

Disembarking, Gemma breathed the sweet fragrance in the air. Jasmine, and an unfamiliar scent. But the sudden intense heat caught her unawares, and the glare of the sun seemed relentless.

Once they disembarked, they hurried across the tarmac to the coolness of the small airport.

"Nikos!"

An older man and woman rushed toward them with big

smiles and open arms.

In seconds, Nikos introduced Gemma to his parents, Stefanos and Maria. They seemed more formal than Gemma expected, but also seemed pleased to meet her.

Before long, they were in their air-conditioned car and heading for their home.

Gemma gazed avidly from the window, trying to see everything. Buildings gleamed sparkling white in the bright sunshine. The roads were wide, with unfamiliar trees lining both sides. Villas were tucked behind high masonry walls, only the tile roofs visible from the street.

As they passed through a shopping district, she was intrigued to see some storefronts with names she'd associated with New York and London, side by side with outdoor displays of local merchandise.

Pylos was obviously a tourist town. People strolled along the sidewalks, and she saw tour buses as they headed out of town.

Gemma continued to stare out the window, charmed by the buildings so different from New York. What else would she find different?

When Stefanos turned between the wide gates of a private estate, Gemma looked eagerly at Nikos' childhood home. The villa was lovely—white with soaring columns and a two-tiered veranda around all sides. Gardens with a profusion of blossoms surrounded the house. Beyond, she glimpsed the sea.

"Welcome to our home," Nikos' mother said, turning to smile politely at Gemma.

"It's beautiful," Gemma replied.

She felt awkward and wished she knew what Nikos' parents really thought of their hasty marriage. So far, they'd been very gracious.

Did they compare her to Katrina? And if so, did they hope this marriage would last?

"I'll show you to your room. You both must be tired from all the travel and the time change. Perhaps you'd care to rest before dinner."

"I was thinking Gemma could take a nap," Nikos said.

Exasperated, Gemma glared at him.

"I'm not tired. I'm too excited. I want to see everything."

"We'll have plenty of time later to see things," he responded.

Gemma frowned. She would not argue with him when they just arrived. But she had something to say once they reached their room.

It was clear that Nikos' parents were aware of the tension building up, but they remained silent.

Her feeling of being totally out of place faded when she saw their rooms. They were warm and inviting. High ceilings gave the illusion that they were larger than their actual size. The far wall was entirely glass, with French doors that opened to a veranda. Had this been the model for his apartment in New York?

The large windows on the adjacent wall overlooked the garden and the sea beyond. She spotted a walkway, partially hidden by towering shrubs she believed led to the beach.

"It's beautiful," she said sincerely, crossing to the windows to gaze at the view.

"I want to walk beside the sea. Go swimming."

She spun around.

"I can't go swimming—I'll feel like a beached whale, plus, I didn't bring a bathing suit."

"Whales don't come as small as you. At this stage, it's hard to even tell you're pregnant. And lack of a suit isn't a problem. Tomorrow we'll go shopping. We'll find something that will fit."

"No, I don't need to go swimming."

"Of course you do. You can't come all the way to Greece and not swim in the sea."

She gave a quick longing glance at the water, then turned back to the room.

"You're right. I need a new suit anyway. I haven't been swimming once since I moved to New York."

She looked at him and placed her hands on her hips.

"There is another matter we need to discuss."

He looked up from the suitcase he started to unpack.

"That sounds ominous."

"You can't speak for me."

"True."

"Then don't be telling people I need a nap. I'm grown up now. If I'm tired, I can say so and do something about it."

He slowly grinned.

Gemma wanted to stomp her foot. His smile caused that fluttering feeling again. Wasn't he taking her seriously?

"I knew the minute the words left my mouth I'd hear about it," he said. "You're right. We had a good night's sleep last night and the flight here was hardly arduous. Change into something comfortable and we'll take the path to the beach. Even if we don't swim today, we can see the water."

"Thank you," she said primly, then laughed. "Maybe this union will last."

"Why wouldn't it, if that's the way we choose?"

"What if your parents don't like me? What if your father doesn't want his son married to another foreigner?" she asked.

What if Nikos realized he'd made a mistake? Was the reason for his distracted air this last week showing that he was already thinking of ways to end their marriage?

Her heart sank. Just when she thought they were drawing closer, he seemed to pull away.

He crossed the room and tilted her chin up with a finger, gazing down into her eyes. Gemma caught her breath, longing to gaze into his eyes for the rest of her life.

"We'll go shopping tomorrow. Today, we'll take it easy. My

father and mother will love you once they get to know you. We'll visit with them after we walk to the sea. You'll love them, I believe, when you get to know them. Tonight we'll all dine on the veranda and enjoy being at my family's home."

She nodded, already growing nervous. She was no good at small talk. What would she find to discuss during dinner?

Two days later, Gemma was frustrated.

She leaned against the railing of their balcony and glared at the sea. Nothing was going as she had thought it would.

Who'd have expected Nikos to be tied up so much with business? Didn't his father trust him? They'd been behind closed doors for hours every day. And tonight there was a reception. An event to welcome their son and his new bride.

She and Maria had little in common. They were cordial at meals, and the older woman had taken her into town one day to shop for the swimsuit Gemma wanted.

Instead of swimming with her husband, she took the path to the beach by herself and tried to enjoy the solitary splendor of the pristine white beach while he was tied up with business.

Tonight she'd meet the neighbors and family friends and smile and try to display how she adored her husband while making sure he never suspected she truly adored him.

She slapped her hand on the railing in frustration. Any thought she had of their learning more about each other had fled. Nikos was more distant than ever. Waiting until she was asleep before coming to bed, he was gone before she awoke in the morning. And they were never alone. What was going on? She understood his wanting to spend time with his parents. But she was feeling totally neglected.

Had being at his home changed his mind? Was he now regretting his hasty marriage to another foreigner? Did he wish to end their agreement and seek true companionship among the women he knew in Greece?

Restless, she pushed away from the railing and headed down the stairs to the garden. Garden was a misnomer. Estate would be more like it, she thought as she reached the area. It was huge, easily covering over ten acres. Winding her way along the sandy pathway, she touched the shrubbery lining the walkway. It grew tall enough to be used in a maze. Alcoves were set every dozen feet, with stone benches and small gurgling fountains. Sitting on one for a moment, she tried to let the soothing sound of the water calm her nerves.

No use. She jumped up and continued walking toward the beach. There was an ornamental gate—for show, not security. It only latched, not locked. She lifted the lever and stepped onto the pristine sand. Not a soul had used the beach when she'd been here since she arrived. It was private to the family, and none of them seemed as enamored with it as she was.

Feeling free for a moment, she ran lightly across the sand until her sandals became drenched with the lapping water. Warm and soft, it seemed to caress her feet. Splashing as she walked, she headed away from the house. She wished Nikos had joined her, but he was once again tied up with his father.

And if she could be at ease with his mother, maybe she wouldn't feel so much like an odd man out. But Maria Petropoulos spoke English hesitantly. And slowly.

Honored she'd even make the effort, Gemma still felt it was a chore, and she hated to put the woman through it. They had little in common. Nikos' mother had no interest in business. And Gemma knew little about taking care of a house as large as theirs.

After two days, Gemma knew the various people who lived in the large house and had even met several neighbors who had stopped by. Most spoke a little English. She felt awkward that she had not tried to learn Greek.

"Gemma."

She turned and her heart skipped, then raced.

Nikos wore loose white trousers. The shirt billowed in the light breeze that danced across the water. She waited, watching him approach, her heart in her throat. He was so gorgeous it was all she could do to keep herself from dashing down the beach and throwing herself into his arms, demanding that he love her as much as she loved him.

"Free for a while?" she asked as he drew near. She knew her place in the scheme of things. Nikos wasn't looking for love.

He was barefoot, and just the sight of his bare feet set her nerves tingling.

"Free until it's time to get ready for the reception." He looked across the sea. "We could go sailing one day if you wish."

"I would. That would be great. But it's also fun to walk along the beach. I haven't seen any shells."

"The beach is raked every few days. Until there is another storm, I doubt you'll find any."

Imagine, they raked the sand. No wonder the wide expanse was so pristine.

"I thought you might be with my mother," he said as they began walking in the direction Gemma had been heading.

"It seems hard for her to speak English."

Had she heard a note of censure? Or just gentle inquiry?

"She likes the chance to practice. Is it too difficult to understand her?"

"Oh, no. She has a beautiful accent, very British and all. Like yours."

She hesitated a moment.

"Ah, but there is something."

"What could we talk about, Nikos? You know I'm not good at small talk, and she and I have nothing in common."

"You can discuss children. She has raised several and would be delighted to offer suggestions. She hesitates to intrude, however."

Gemma swung around and stared at him. "You told them about the baby?"

Chapter Ten

Nikos nodded. "It is not something that can be kept a secret, you know."

"What did they say? Are they horrified? Oh, Nikos, I wish you'd waited until after we returned home."

"They're my parents, Gemma. I couldn't keep such an event from them. Besides, my mother guessed."

"What did they say?"

He drew a deep breath, remembering the scene with his father. He wouldn't like to repeat such conversation, but what was done was done.

"My mother loves babies. She'll be delighted."

"Will be? When? Obviously not now."

"Well, they're concerned because the baby is not mine."

"I bet your father threw a fit."

He smiled slightly and shook his head.

"Not precisely. He's not one given to throwing fits."

But his temper was not something Nikos liked to run up against often.

"You know what I mean," she said impatiently. "I bet

they're furious. Do they want me to leave?"

"Gemma, they are hosting a reception tonight for the express purpose of introducing you to our friends and other family members. How could they want you to leave?"

"I feel funny seeing them again. I bet they wish the baby was yours."

"Yes, they do. I won't hide that from you."

"Well, I don't blame them, I wish—"

She halted and looked horrified.

"What? Is something wrong?"

Without thinking, he reached for her, drawing her into his embrace.

"What is it, Gemma?"

"Nothing. The baby gave an odd kick, that's all."

"Ah. Can I feel him kick?"

"What?"

Gemma pushed against his chest, but Nikos refused to release her. He enjoyed holding Gemma. Enjoyed being with her. These last few days couldn't have been easy for her left alone so much, but his father wanted to be brought up to speed on the various enterprises in America. And both evenings, when he'd retired, she'd already been sound asleep.

Slowly, she turned in his embrace and took one of his hands, pressing it against the slight swelling of her abdomen. Nikos was aware of the warmth beneath his palm, of her scent filling his senses, of her hair blowing against his cheek when he leaned closer.

"It could be a girl," she said.

Then, a slight movement beneath his palm.

"There, did you feel that?" she asked.

Touched beyond belief, he nodded and held still, longing to feel that flutter of life again. Twice more he felt something.

"So he's going to be a soccer player."

"Or ballet dancer," she murmured, resting against his chest.

"This is a special gift you have given me, Gemma. Thank you."

"No Nikos, you've given me a special gift. One for which I will always be grateful."

He stepped back, annoyed at her sentiments.

"I don't want your gratitude," he said sharply.

She looked at him for a long moment, then nodded. "Very well," she said stiffly. She hesitated a moment, then turned to retrace her steps. "I'm feeling tired and think I should rest this afternoon. We'll be up late tonight."

Nikos stood and watched her walk back toward the villa. Her head was high and her shoulders back, but he had the feeling she wasn't as confident as she appeared.

For a long moment, he watched her walk away. She had not asked him to accompany her, had not sought his company.

Was that to be the way of their marriage? Parallel lives, never connecting, never intersecting.

Gemma pushed through the gate and headed up the sandy path. Flouncing down on one of the benches, she glared at the shrubbery opposite. Things were not going well, and she hadn't a clue what to do about it.

"Madam?"

Turning, she saw Stefanos' assistant. What was his name? Xander.

"Hello."

"I saw you come in from a walk on the beach. You left Nikos there."

"Yes."

She wasn't about to let anyone know of her frustrations—especially an aide to Nikos' father. She already knew his father didn't approve. No sense feeding that disapproval.

"Nikos is Stefanos' oldest son. He is heir to his father's holdings. His place will be here in Pylos when his fathers retires or dies. While that may not be for many years, Nikos will need to step up with the help and support of his family."

Gemma nodded. "Do you think I wouldn't move here when that time comes?"

"You know nothing about our country, our customs, our traditions. I suspect you simply saw a wealthy man, captivated him with your wiles and beguiled him into marriage. This isn't what his father wished for him. But it is not too late to change things. Dissolve this absurd marriage and I'll see that you have ample funds to live the life you hoped to live with Nikos—

better, for you won't have to move here."

"There's not enough money in the world," she said scornfully.

"You prefer the prestige of being married to him, is that it?"

"No. Money only buys things. I'm not a thing and I'm not interested in money. If his father thought to buy me off, too bad. I'm not leaving Nikos."

"We can make things very uncomfortable for you."

Gemma had had enough. She leaped to her feet, placed her hands on her hips, and glared at him.

"Doesn't matter. It's Nikos who matters, not his father. If Nikos tells me to leave, I will. But I won't go unless he's the one to tell me."

"I did not say I come from his father. Did you ever consider that I might be here from Nikos directly?" Xander asked slowly.

"Ha. If Nikos didn't like the arrangement, he'd let me know in no uncertain terms. He's the one who proposed this crazy marriage. I expect he'll tell me if he tires of it. He doesn't need some gofer to do that."

But the doubts built. Hadn't she noticed he'd pulled away in the last several days? Was he regretting their hasty alliance? Had he sought to avoid a scene by sending Xander?

"A besotted woman thinks she can wrap a man around her finger. Better take the offer while it's still available, or you'll be out with nothing."

"Besotted." She wanted to scream with frustration. "I may love the man, but I'm not besotted. He isn't perfect. He's arrogant and always ordering things to suit him. Like this marriage."

"Love?" Xander sounded perplexed. "What does that have to do with marriage? Nikos needs a woman of his own country to give him the support he'll need when he returns to Greece to live."

"I know enough about love to know he also needs someone on his side, someone who cares about him and what he's thinking and feeling, and not for some society thing. He doesn't need a woman just because of her place of birth. He had his chance to meet someone here, yet he chose me. So you march inside and let his father know I'm not leaving unless Nikos tells me to."

Xander hesitated a moment, then calmly inclined his head. "You know where to find me if you change your mind."

Furious, Gemma watched him walk away as if he had not a care in the world. Had he come from Nikos? Had being in his own country changed Nikos' mind about staying with her?

He'd made no moves to increase their intimacy—did that prove he was losing interest?

She turned and headed back toward the beach, then saw Nikos when she reached the gate. Hoping for a moment to calm her nerves, she waited for him, her anger growing as he took his time. Anger and suspicions that maybe Xander had been telling the truth. Maybe he *had* come from Nikos.

"I want to speak to you," she said when he drew close.

"About?"

Nikos paused by the gate and studied her. She knew she was flushed with the anger that threatened to overwhelm her. But that couldn't be helped. She needed answers now.

"About an attempted bribe to end our marriage."

"What are you talking about?"

He seemed surprised at her announcement.

"Who has mentioned a bribe? Or even hinted at ending the marriage?"

"Your father's assistant. He suggested he came from you, but I don't believe him. At least, I don't think I do. He said you wanted to end our marriage and would give me lots of money to go."

"Ah. And your response?" Nikos waited politely, his gaze never leaving hers.

"I told him I wasn't for sale. If you wish to end this relationship, you come right out and tell me. Otherwise, it sticks."

Without waiting for a response, she whirled around and almost ran to the stairs leading to their balcony.

She was almost shaking with nerves. Had she made another mistake, a worse one than with James? The emotion she felt for that man had faded, seemed paltry compared to the intensity of her love for Nikos. But her track record wasn't great with men. Had she misread the signs, trying to convince herself that Nikos wanted her as much as she wanted him?

Several hours later, Gemma twisted this way and that as she looked at herself in the mirror, wondering if she should wear the dress or not. It had looked elegant and sophisticated in New York. But with the heightened modesty prevalent among the women she'd met since arriving in Greece, she wondered if it was too daring.

The gown brushed her ankles as she walked, the soft pale yellow chiffon falling from the clip at her left shoulder. The right was bare. Both arms were bare and lightly tanned from her days on the beach. The loose-fitting garment hid all signs of her pregnancy and looked feminine and alluring.

Tilting her head slightly, she narrowed her eyes.

Alluring?

Would Nikos find her alluring?

Slowly, she practiced a smile. She'd loved to be sultry and sexy, mysterious and intriguing. But then she sighed. She looked like she always did—just plain old Gemma Green, all dressed up for the ball.

Nikos knocked on the partially open door. He stepped inside, looking splendid in the white dinner jacket. His dark hair gleamed in the light. For a moment Gemma thought a matching light gleamed in his eyes. But she must have been imagining it.

Flustered by her outburst by the gate, she was unsure how to greet him. He hadn't confirmed nor denied his involvement with the bribe. And despite her fine words about wanting to know, she hesitated to push the issue.

What would she do if he walked away?

Trying to ignore the rapid beat of her heart, she raised her chin. She refused to give way to fear. What happened, happened, and she'd have to deal with it.

"Will this do?" she asked. "It's not too daring, is it?"

Do you wish to end our marriage?

He shook his head.

"My mother buys her gowns in Paris. A direct influence of her sister-in-law, Allessandros's mother. The party will be like any other you've attended. Most of the guests speak some English and will do so in your presence."

"I guess I'm ready, then," she muttered, touching her hair, nervous with him watching her.

How she wished Nikos had firmly denied any involvement in the bribe. She wished he'd reaffirm his commitment to their marriage. Say something to end this uncertainty.

Instead of attending the reception, she wished he'd sweep her into his arms and carry her off to a romantic retreat. She'd love to spend the evening watching the sunset over the sea, feel the clear air against her skin. Make love beneath a blanket of brilliant stars.

Instead, tonight she had to endure yet another gathering where she'd feel insecure and uncertain. And Nikos did nothing to help.

"You look lovely."

The warmth of his compliment surprised her. Meeting his eyes in the mirror, she smiled shyly.

"Thank you."

"Shall we?"

Nikos offered his hand and Gemma slipped hers into it. The heat from his palm warmed hers. Taking a deep breath, she grew determined to do her very best to not let Nikos down. He'd done so much for her, she wanted to make sure he never regretted it.

If she couldn't have his love, she'd make sure she kept his respect.

Nikos scanned the ballroom some time later. He didn't see Gemma and wondered where she'd gotten to. His mother had invited half the country, he thought with wry amusement. And he felt as if he'd talked to everyone present.

Many met Katrina when they'd been together. And several expressed their surprise that he'd married another foreigner.

Not that it mattered. He'd choose his own wife.

Once again, he searched the room. Maybe she went outside. Slowly he made his way to the veranda. Couples walked in the evening coolness, and a few guests had gathered in a small group, sharing laughter and conversation.

"Looking for your bride?" his cousin Emil asked.

"Have you seen her?"

Emil nodded toward the garden. "She and Cosmo walked in that direction a few moments ago. She's very unlike Katrina, cousin."

Nikos looked at him. "To the good or bad?"

"Much to the good. I wish you all happiness."

Nikos nodded and headed in the direction Emil had indicated. The path looked deserted. At the intersection with another, he heard voices. Slowly he turned, drawing closer. He could hear them clearly before he could see them.

"I knew Katrina well. Are you as enchanting and generous as she?"

"What does that mean?" Gemma asked.

"She was, shall we say, generous with her favors. I wonder if Nikos' present wife is as generous."

Nikos stopped dead, anger slowly building. How dare Cosmo make such a remark to his wife. Nikos' hands fisted, and he moved forward. He'd make the man regret he ever entertained such a thought, much less voiced it.

But Gemma's voice stopped him.

"I've got news for you, buster. Katrina and I are nothing alike. So take your hands off me before I bop you one."

"I like fire in a woman."

"Yes, well, so does Nikos. And I suspect he isn't one to share. Not that I'd ever be tempted. I love my husband, and I find every other man on the planet a pale imitation. If you want to walk out of here, take a hike now before you end up singing soprano."

"A misunderstanding. I apologize for the misunderstanding."

Nikos heard the man walk away and rounded the path way to join Gemma.

"I didn't realize I had such an intimidating wife," Nikos said when she looked at him.

Nikos let out his pent-up breath as he looked at Gemma. His heart pounded.

"Hi Nikos," she said.

He liked the flustered look about her. Gone was the cool, serene personal assistant he was used to seeing every day. Before him stood a woman with sparkling eyes and wearing a dress designed to drive a man mad.

"I couldn't help overhearing your altercation with Cosmo."

"Honestly, I can't believe the man thought I'd want to make out in the garden with him. What an ego."

She tried to brush past Nikos.

"Time to return to the party, I guess."

"In a moment. I heard you tell him you loved me."

She studied one of the flowering bushes highlighted by the garden lights. "Mmm."

He reached out and tilted her chin until she looked up and

met his gaze.

"Is it true?"

She swallowed. He watched the movement of her throat and thought about how he'd like to kiss her there.

"Yes, it's true. But I won't let it change anything. I remember the terms of our agreement."

"Ah."

He was silent a long moment, staring into her eyes, watching them change from defiant to apprehensive.

"If you still want to stay married," she said slowly.

"Why wouldn't I?"

"I don't know. Xander had a point. Others probably think I'm like Katrina—like that man did." She raised her chin. "But I'm not."

"No, Gemma, you're most certainly not."

"So we carry on?"

She held her breath. *Please say yes.*

"Actually, an excellent negotiator knows when to change things," he murmured, drawing her into his arms. "I believe it's time to change the terms of our marriage agreement."

"You do?" Her eyes grew wide. "How?"

"I want to make it real."

"Oh," was all she had time to say before his mouth came down on hers.

Nikos felt the blood sing in his veins. *She loves me.* It was more than he expected or deserved.

Long moments later the sound of voices intruded. Nikos broke the kiss, grabbed her hand, and headed away from the house.

"That's the problem with parties—there's no privacy."

Gemma kept pace, her hand gripping his. When they reached the gate, Nikos urged her through to the pristine white sand.

"Are you sure, Nikos?"

He ran his finger along her cheek, beneath her jaw, savoring the silky texture of her skin. His longing to make her his grew with each passing moment.

"I think I'd like ties and promises if they kept you with me forever."

She smiled and he smiled back, feeling the relief flow through him.

"I love you, Gemma Petropoulos. I think I realized it the day in the department store when you worried about what I was getting out of our arrangement. I think that is the first time anyone ever worried about my benefits. I know it in my heart and soul—you are all I need and want. You will be all I need for the rest of my life."

"Oh, Nikos."

She flung herself into his arms, encircling his neck with hers and hugging him tightly.

"I love you so much. I thought you only married me for expediency, and I vowed I'd never give you a reason to regret it. But I think I've loved you for ages. I knew for sure when we stayed at Allessandros'."

He relished the sensation of her soft body against the length of his.

"I thought you felt gratitude."

She shook her head. "I do, but that's only part of it. Mostly I love you."

"Overbearing and arrogant as I am?" he murmured, his lips trailing kissed along her sweet skin.

She nodded.

"You, on a bad day, are still better than any other man in the world on his best day," she whispered. "But are you sure? I don't want to cause a problem in your family."

"My mother already loves you. My father shall come around. Especially when he sees how happy you make me. But I'm not here to talk about them, only about us. Shall we steal away tonight, lose ourselves in all Greece has to offer, and have that honeymoon Elise has been lecturing me about?"

She gave a gurgle of laughter.

"I can't see Elise lecturing anyone, especially you."

"Ah, perhaps they were more like strong hints. But you didn't answer my question."

Gemma's eyes drifted shut.

"I'd love nothing better."

Nikos was not a man to resist a blatant invitation. His mouth closed over hers again and he kissed his wife with all the love in his heart. Tomorrow he'd show her the beauty of Greece. They'd spend a week alone, truly beginning their lives together. And when it was time, they'd return to their home in New York stronger than ever in their marriage—because of the endless ties of love.

Epilogue

"It's a girl," the doctor said as the lusty cries filled the birthing room.

"We have a daughter," Nikos said with satisfaction.

Gemma promptly burst into tears. She clung to her husband's hand and tried to smile through the tears.

"Is she all right?" she asked.

"Looks perfect," the doctor said, laying the baby on Gemma's stomach. Nikos reached out to run a finger down her cheek, and she stopped crying, her wide infant eyes turning to him.

"She's beautiful," he murmured. "Just like her mother."

Gemma blinked furiously, trying to see clearly. "Looks tiny and red and—"

"Hush, love. She'll be as beautiful as you."

Nikos leaned over to kiss her, his fingers lacing through hers.

"Or almost. I doubt anyone will ever be that lovely."

Gemma smiled and tightened her grip. "I love you," she said.

"I love you and Alicia."

"Is that what we decided we'll call her?"

"Unless you prefer another name. As you said when suggesting Alicia, it's in memory of your mother. We can name our next daughter for my mother. My parents are eager for us to visit so they can see Alicia and you."

"I'm glad they've accepted me."

"Accepted? Darling, they love you for yourself and because you've made me so happy."

"Even your father?"

"Even him. Shall we go for a quick visit to Greece as soon as you and our daughter are ready, so we can show her off?"

"Whatever you say," Gemma said, fascinated by the baby, who was now looking around as if taking in the brand-new world she'd just entered.

"We'll clean her up and bring her to you in a few minutes," the nurse said briskly, wrapping a warm blanket around the infant and whisking her away.

"Is this new docility going to continue?" Nikos asked to distract her when he saw the look on her face at the departure of her new daughter.

"What?" She looked at him. "What docility?"

"Whatever I say?"

"That's temporary until I'm in fighting shape again."

"But we rarely fight," he said, smiling in memory of some

of the terrific *discussions* they'd had. And the making up afterward.

She laughed and reached up to pull him closer.

"I love you, Nikos. You've made my life perfect."

"Ah, Gemma, only God is perfect. But you and I together come pretty darn close."

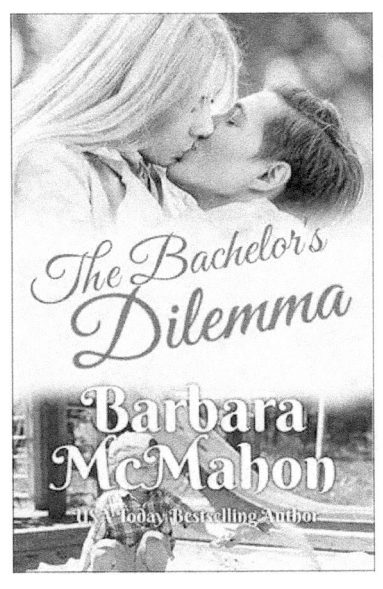

Did you enjoy this story?
If so, you may enjoy THE BACHELOR'S DILEMMA,
Book Four in the Making a Family Series.

For a complete list of Barbara's books, visit her website at
www.barbaramcmahon.com/books.

If you liked MARRIAGE MASQUERADE book,
please consider leaving a review.